A Candlelight Ecstasy Romance

"WHAT HAPPENED? I FEEL LIKE I'VE BEEN HIT WITH A SLEDGEHAMMER," BYRON MUTTERED.

China glanced away. "I thought you were a burglar. I hit you with the pitcher of flowers that was on the coffee table."

Byron stared at her. "You did *what?*" He shook his head, then reached up to touch it. "I don't remember a thing, but I've got a devil of a headache."

Before China could explain again and apologize, Byron spotted his clothes scattered around the floor. He raised the coverlet to peer down at his nude body.

"China, you naughty girl," he drawled. "You've stripped me—and heaven knows what else. You didn't have to knock me out to do this. We could have talked about it. I'm sure we could have worked something out so that we both could have enjoyed it."

"I see that you've recovered," China said dryly, but she could feel the color rising to her face.

CANDLELIGHT ECSTASY ROMANCES®

250 SUMMER WINE, *Alexis Hill Jordan*
251 NO LOVE LOST, *Eleanor Woods*
252 A MATTER OF JUDGMENT, *Emily Elliott*
253 GOLDEN VOWS, *Karen Whittenburg*
254 AN EXPERT'S ADVICE, *Joanne Bremer*
255 A RISK WORTH TAKING, *Jan Stuart*
256 GAME PLAN, *Sara Jennings*
257 WITH EACH PASSING HOUR, *Emma Bennett*
258 PROMISE OF SPRING, *Jean Hager*
259 TENDER AWAKENING, *Alison Tyler*
260 DESPERATE YEARNING, *Dallas Hamlin*
261 GIVE AND TAKE, *Sheila Paulos*
262 AN UNFORGETTABLE CARESS, *Donna Kimel Vitek*
263 TOMORROW WILL COME, *Megan Lane*
264 RUN TO RAPTURE, *Margot Prince*
265 LOVE'S SECRET GARDEN, *Nona Gamel*
266 WINNER TAKES ALL, *Cathie Linz*
267 A WINNING COMBINATION, *Lori Copeland*
268 A COMPROMISING PASSION, *Nell Kincaid*
269 TAKE MY HAND, *Anna Hudson*
270 HIGH STAKES, *Eleanor Woods*
271 SERENA'S MAGIC, *Heather Graham*
272 A DARING ALLIANCE, *Alison Tyler*
273 SCATTERED ROSES, *Jo Calloway*
274 WITH ALL MY HEART, *Emma Bennett*
275 JUST CALL MY NAME, *Dorothy Ann Bernard*
276 THE PERFECT AFFAIR, *Lynn Patrick*
277 ONE IN A MILLION, *Joan Grove*
278 HAPPILY EVER AFTER, *Barbara Andrews*
279 SINNER AND SAINT, *Prudence Martin*
280 RIVER RAPTURE, *Patricia Markham*
281 MATCH MADE IN HEAVEN, *Malissa Carroll*
282 TO REMEMBER LOVE, *Jo Calloway*
283 EVER A SONG, *Karen Wittenburg*
284 CASANOVA'S MASTER, *Anne Silverlock*
285 PASSIONATE ULTIMATUM, *Emma Bennett*
286 A PRIZE CATCH, *Anna Hudson*
287 LOVE NOT THE ENEMY, *Sara Jennings*
288 SUMMER FLING, *Natalie Stone*
289 AMBER PERSUASION, *Linda Vail*

LIVE TOGETHER AS STRANGERS

Megan Lane

A CANDLELIGHT ECSTASY ROMANCE®

*To Dr. Hammarlund, for his kindness;
to Dr. Stoddard in appreciation
for his interest and compassion
for exotic birds and those
of us who have them; and
to my inspiration—*

Published by
Dell Publishing Co., Inc.
1 Dag Hammarskjold Plaza
New York, New York 10017

ISBN: 0-440-14744-1

Printed in the United States of America
First printing—December 1984

To Our Readers:

We have been delighted with your enthusiastic response to Candlelight Ecstasy Romances®, and we thank you for the interest you have shown in this exciting series.

In the upcoming months we will continue to present the distinctive, sensuous love stories you have come to expect only from Ecstasy. We look forward to bringing you many more books from your favorite authors and also the very finest work from new authors of contemporary romantic fiction.

As always, we are striving to present the unique, absorbing love stories that you enjoy most—books that are more than ordinary romance.

Your suggestions and comments are always welcome. Please write to us at the address below.

Sincerely,

The Editors
Candlelight Romances
1 Dag Hammarskjold Plaza
New York, New York 10017

CHAPTER ONE

Muttering and cursing, China Castleberry dragged her belongings from the compact car. It was a dreadful northern California night, with the rain pouring down and the wind blowing. She had endured a harrowing drive up the twisting coastal route from southern California to this isolated ranch hidden in the craggy hills of Big Sur, and she had never been so glad to reach a house in her life. It was only a rough-hewn pine cabin, but tonight it looked like heaven.

She was relieved to see that the old couple who had once been her grandparents' ranch hands had left a light burning for her. She had called and told them she would be arriving late, but it was much later than she had expected. In the sudden downpour she had been forced to take extreme care in driving the tortuous road that wrapped around the mountainsides, and at all times she had been aware of the danger of going over a cliff and tumbling into the savage sea below the highway.

But, thank God, that was behind her now. She had even taken the correct road to get to the ranch—always a trick, even in daylight, for the property was so well hidden and so sequestered that one had to know exactly where one was going to find it.

"Some honeymoon," she murmured sourly to herself as the rain beat against her and the blustering wind tore at her coat. She glanced at the dark, menacing sky. "Thanks a lot for the beautiful weather," she said, shaking her fist.

The car door was still standing open, and Blue, China's blue-fronted Amazon parrot, began to imitate his mistress, muttering in a voice remarkably like her own. "Thanks a lot," he repeated, then he squawked irritably, annoyed at being left in the car.

"Just a minute," she said soothingly, setting her new suitcase down on the wet driveway. It was so dark that she could hardly see anything against the gravel driveway leading to the cabin, but she knew that water was running down it, soaking her shoes. She hadn't wanted to try to get the car into the narrow garage in the dark, so she would leave it here until morning. She reached into the back to get the cover to Blue's cage, then slipped it over the grumbling bird. "Lights out!" he cried noisily, and China managed to smile in spite of her difficulties.

It was amazing that she *could* smile. The weather was awful, and she was still recovering from Dereck's deceit and the second cancellation of their wedding plans. Besides, she knew she would be assaulted by a thousand sweet memories of Granny Castleberry when she went into the old cabin, memories that were sure to bring tears to her eyes.

She and her grandmother had shared some very special times here, especially after Gramps had died and there were only the two of them, making women's talk on the rare occasions when they could share a long weekend. China had always loved this place; it was her retreat from the world. She had often come here to commune with nature, as Granny did, and to renew herself. And sometimes just to have Granny give her some practical advice and good commonsense rules to live by.

She always went away with a better perspective on life. The peace she found at the cabin allowed her to deal with the world she had to work in. Being in Big Sur was so different from the hectic pace of Palm Springs, and if China could ever afford to, she would love to live here all the time, just as her grandmother had.

She would be eternally grateful that her grandmother had left the cabin to her. She had promised herself that she would care for it and the land and love it as had her Granny. And when—if —she ever had children, she would leave it to them to enjoy as she and her family had.

Her thoughts caused her to feel a little sad. There would be no Granny this time to reassure her about her broken engagement, to tell her that all things worked for the best. There

8

would be no Granny to distract her from the pain that ran rampant in her heart with all-too-well-remembered familiarity.

Still, this was the best place for her, and she was looking forward to her two weeks here. At home she would be subjected to all kinds of expressions of surprise and pity. She didn't want the sympathetic stares of her friends and relatives.

This wasn't England, Scotland, Ireland, and Wales, as she had intended, but despite her vows to do so, she hadn't been able to persuade herself to go on alone. She had planned that trip—her honeymoon trip with Dereck—and she wanted to see those places with someone she loved. Big Sur would have to do instead, and she knew that having some time to herself in this solitary place would do her a world of good. But how she would love to see her grandmother. How very good it would be to hug the old woman and sit with her in the kitchen, drinking coffee and talking.

Granny had been dead less than three months, and China missed her intensely, although she had lived many hours away from the brooding Big Sur area and had rarely had a chance to visit. Her father had been raised here on this land, but his career had taken him into the Palm Springs area. Gramps and Granny had stayed on the ranch, refusing all of James Castleberry's attempts to lure them away.

"Thanks a lot," Blue muttered sourly when a gust of wind ripped at his cover, exposing him to the chilly air.

"All right, all right," China said, picking his cage up in one hand and her suitcase in the other. She reached back and kicked the door closed with a well-shod foot, then cursed as her shoulder bag tumbled down her arm to crash against the bird cage.

"Thanks a lot," Blue repeated.

"Will you shut up," China muttered. "I have enough problems without your sarcasm."

The bird became more subdued as China walked toward the house, somehow managing to locate the flower-lined path, but she knew it wasn't because he was obeying her. He was in motion, and he wasn't quite sure what to expect now.

The wind lashed out at them again, and China felt as if she were the only person alive and out in the bad weather tonight. Few people lived in the area, and even fewer in this section.

9

Gramps and Granny had once raised cattle, loving the rugged terrain and inaccessibility of their fifty-acre ranch.

Gradually they had sold off all their stock and more and more of their land; now there were several other landowners here, but none of their homes were visible in the darkness. The houses were few and far apart, most of them suspended precariously over the cliffs' edges, giving them a dramatic view of the battering sea below.

Only Karly and Randolph Davis lived close enough for their house to be seen; a small cabin, it was an even simpler version of the Castleberry home, built down in the midst of the trees behind the main house. They had been granted the right to stay on the land as long as they lived, in return for their faithful care of Granny after Gramps had died. China was grateful they were there, for now they took care of the cabin for her.

Finally she stepped up on the porch and set her burdens down so that she could rummage in her purse for the door key. "At last," she said, holding it up triumphantly. She shoved the key into the door and opened it. There was a single dim light on in the living room, and China smiled. Karly Davis must have left it on for her.

After setting Blue's cage down on the floor and shutting the door, China headed toward the fireplace, where the last embers of a fire still glowed. How thoughtful of the Davises, she told herself. She would build it up again if there were wood on the hearth.

"What the hell—?"

China spun around in fright, her heart pounding alarmingly at the sound of the man's voice. He switched the three-intensity lamp to its brightest, flooding the room with light. China stared at him in shocked surprise, seeing his angry slate-colored eyes and his light blond curls. He was long and lean and wiry-looking. She could see that perfectly well, for he was barely dressed. She glanced at the woman who had been freed from his arms. The redhead struggled to sit up, tugging modestly at her robe as she stared suspiciously from the man to China.

Despite her astonishment, China could see that the woman was a beauty. Voluptuous breasts were spilling from the opening in the forest-green silk dressing gown she wore, and her

10

legs, which moments ago had been entwined with the man's hairy ones, were smooth and shapely. Her lipstick was gone, no doubt kissed away, China thought wryly.

"What are you doing in here?" the blond man demanded, unfolding himself from the couch. Gathering his short brown robe to his muscled body, he tied the belt around his narrow waist, and China couldn't keep her eyes from following the motion. He was taller than she had thought at first, and he seemed overpowering in spite of his wiry build as he towered over her own considerable five-foot-nine-inch height.

For a moment she wondered if she were in the wrong house, but of course that was ridiculous. She had opened the door with her key. Yet, *he* was asking *her* what she was doing here. It was outrageous! She brushed at masses of wavy black hair, now clinging damply to her shoulders, wet from the rain.

"Me? The question is what are you two doing in my house?" she demanded, letting her gaze encompass the redhead, who was staring at her as if she had deliberately walked in on them in order to catch them like this.

China found herself thinking that Granny would turn over in her grave if she saw this sight—Granny, who had remained virtuous and pristine, a lovely old-fashioned lady sheltered from the real world and changing times by Grampa Castleberry and the seclusion of the ranch. She had missed the sexual revolution altogether, and lack of television and radio had shielded her from the realities of a promiscuous time and age.

The area was so rural and segregated that some places had only recently gotten electricity, and television reception was so bad that the cabin still didn't have one. Granny and Gramps had lived here in a world of their own. China doubted that the old Victorian couch upon which the red-haired beauty sat had ever known such carrying-on before.

"Your house?" he repeated as though she were insane. "This happens to be my house. Now, I don't know if you lost your way in the rain or just what your problem is, and frankly I don't care. Kindly be on your way."

"Mr.—whatever your name is," China said tartly, instantly annoyed with his dismissing tone, "you happen to be in *my* house! Now, let me say the same to you: I don't care how you came to be here, but *you*'d best be on your way. I have no idea who let you in or why. I realize the house has been standing vacant for the past three months, but I am the legal owner, so please take your—your possessions," she said, looking at the other woman, "and go."

She could feel her temper rise. The last thing she had expected tonight was to find a man and a woman here in this cabin, making love! If she weren't so weary and unhappy, it would almost be laughable; she had come here to escape her own aborted love life and had walked right in on two strangers wrapped up in each other's arms.

Suddenly there was a terrible ruckus as the biggest black cat China had ever seen leaped down from a high-backed chair and charged Blue's cage, attacking full force, obviously having spied the bird peeking from under the cover.

Just as quickly, China closed the distance between her and the cat and struggled to pry it from the cage, where it was busy trying to reach in between the thin bars to get at Blue. The panicked bird was giving a soft clucking cry of distress, and China was furious. The determined cat clung to the cover with its claws, and China was literally helpless to rescue Blue. In a fury she turned toward the man.

"Get this damned cat off this cage before my parrot dies of fright!" she demanded.

She conceded that he at least had the decency to do as she asked, moving quickly and agilely to drag the black beast off by the scruff of its neck. China bent down and lifted the cage, placing it on the nearest table, then took off the cover, opened the door, and took the trembling parrot, perched on her finger, out of the cage. "It's all right," she said, crooning softly as she kissed his beak. "It's all right. You're okay."

"He damned well won't be if you don't put him back in there and get the hell out of here," the man said.

China glanced back to see him still holding the struggling cat, claws bared, by the back of the neck. Immediately she put Blue back in his cage and shut the door. Then she recovered it and took it into her granny's bedroom. When she had turned on the light, she tried not to notice the two suitcases side by side, open on the bed, one brown, one pink. She set Blue on the old-fashioned bureau, then firmly closed the door.

She was angry now. She was tired. And she was very curious. "I really can't believe this is happening," she muttered to herself. "My luck just can't be this bad." Striding toward the couple, who now stood in front of the dying fire, she said, "I'll tell you once more—get out of here. I don't know what you think you're doing here"—she glanced away; it was quite obvious what they were doing here—"but just get out! Now, before I call the police."

The man shrugged lazily. "Call them. I'd prefer it. Then you'll be on your way."

"Didn't you hear what I said?" China asked. "I own this house. You have no right being here!"

The man gave her such an indulgent smile that she wanted to slap his face. "Sorry to disappoint you," he said mockingly, "but I own the house. Now, I don't know who *you* are, but I'm Byron Scott. Mrs. Colleen Castleberry left this house to me when she died three months ago. *I*'m the legal owner."

For a moment China stared at him, stunned, her milky-white skin even paler. What was he talking about? Granny was her father's mother. China herself had inherited the house.

"I beg your pardon," she murmured thickly, "but I happen to be China Castleberry, Colleen Castleberry's granddaughter. I inherited this house."

The redhead, clearly not at all pleased by recent developments, turned angrily to Byron. "What's going on here?" she demanded. "Just who is this woman and why has she come? I came here with you expecting some privacy. I don't like this one little bit!"

"Neither do I," Byron assured her. "Of course I didn't expect anyone else."

"Well, do you think *I* anticipated walking in here and finding *you two?*" China flung at them. "This is my grandmother's house!"

Frowning a little, the man studied China for a moment. So this was the elusive granddaughter Colleen had spoken so fondly of—the only grandchild the old lady had had—and she hadn't bothered to come around when her granny was alive. It was a pet peeve of his, families neglecting their elderly relatives. When Gene Castleberry was still living, the granddaughter's absence had irritated Byron, but it hadn't angered him like it did when Colleen had been left all alone. He had been surprised but pleased when Colleen had cut the girl out of her will—not that he had wanted the house himself, but because of the principle involved. And he would make some attempt to honor the old woman's wishes.

His gray eyes assessed China boldly; he hadn't expected her to look as she did. There was very little of her grandmother's appearance in her. His gaze roved over her, taking in her brown eyes, dark hair, and long, shapely body. She was wearing a beige all-weather coat over a chic brown dress. Her feet were encased in wet, rich-looking beige pumps. His appraisal went the length of her long legs, and China resisted the urge to wrap her coat more tightly around herself.

She returned the man's frank gaze, refusing to be intimidated by a stranger, no matter what he thought his rights here were. He was handsome, she conceded, almost too handsome with his pale blond curls, his large gray eyes, fringed by thick gold lashes, and his finely chiseled features. She had never found blond men very attractive, she told herself, but this one had a certain something. She brushed at the ridiculous thought. She couldn't care less about the man's looks. She just wanted him out of here.

"I trust you're aware that you don't inherit merely because you're a relative," Byron said thoughtfully, as though he were talking to someone lacking in mental powers.

"I certainly do," China muttered crossly. "I inherited because Granny left a will saying that the house belongs to me, the legal heir."

She watched as Byron ran long, slender fingers through his curls, ruffling them even more than they had been, and she found herself thinking that the redhead must have done that a moment ago.

"Are you telling the truth?" he demanded suddenly.

"Why would I lie?" she retorted. She watched as he and the other woman exchanged a look. "Listen," China said, "why don't you just get out of here tonight and tomorrow I'll have

14

the lawyer contact you. He lives in Monterey and he'll be happy to confirm my ownership."

"Lloyd Thomas?"

China nodded. "Yes, that's his name. He's been my grandparents' lawyer for as long as I can remember."

"And my father's," Byron stated. He glanced at the redhead again, then motioned to China. "China Castleberry, this is Marlene Jergens."

The two women nodded in barely civil acknowledgment of each other.

"Why don't we sit down and talk about this?" Byron said. "It's late. We're all tired and obviously there's some mistake."

"What do you mean?" China asked.

Byron sighed. "I have heard of you, now that you remind me. Your granny spoke of you often in fact—Che-Che, I believe, was the fond endearment," he said dryly.

China felt a blush rise to her ivory cheeks. Yes, he certainly had heard her granny speak of her. She had tried tirelessly to break Granny Castleberry of that silly nickname, but it had proved futile. When China had been a child, she had had trouble with her name, stumbling over it and converting it into Che-Che. Granny had adopted it and never called her anything else.

Reluctantly, China followed the couple to the couch, but she chose the chair the cat had vacated. Marlene sat stiffly on the edge of the couch, her head held high, and China told herself that at least the woman had enough dignity to be embarrassed at being discovered in this position.

Byron was still holding the beast, stroking its fur gently, and China found her gaze drawn to the movement, which was somehow seductive. She was mesmerized by the sight of the man's long, lean fingers fanning out against the richness of the black fur, rhythmically smoothing it. Finally she looked away, gazing at an ornate gray-pottery pitcher that was filled with wildflowers.

As if to let her know he had noticed her staring, Byron murmured, "This is Demon. He was my mother's cat, and when she died I inherited him."

Then he startled her by saying, "I also inherited this house from your Granny Castleberry." At the shocked expression on

15

her face, he continued. "I don't know what's going on here either. I know she wasn't senile, and I know that the will leaving the house to me is valid. I know Lloyd Thomas well—have all my life. He's my father's friend. They both live in Monterey, as did I before I moved to Santa Monica."

China had come here to escape the shambles of her engagement, to try to put her life back in order, and just look what she had found. She was stunned by the unexpectedness of Byron Scott's being here with this woman. It seemed wrong for him to defile this house in this manner. He was ruining the peace and comfort and isolation that had been its best qualities. He was cheapening it and all that it had stood for in China's mind.

"I don't understand either," she said, trying to speak rationally, "but I've driven all the way from Palm Springs and I want to get some sleep. Can't you and Miss Jergens go to her place tonight? I'm sure we can work this out in the morning with the lawyer."

China hadn't yet met the lawyer who was handling her grandmother's estate, but after she had received the letter telling her she had inherited the cabin, she had called to say she would wrap up the legal formalities the next time she came to Big Sur. This was her first trip since Granny's death, and she was planning to make an appointment to see Mr. Thomas, but she certainly hadn't had any reason to think the matter was urgent—until now.

Byron glanced at Marlene. "Miss Jergens came with me from Santa Monica. We're tired too. Perhaps you could find other lodging since we arrived first."

China couldn't help but think they hadn't looked tired when she had discovered them, but she dismissed the thought. "I don't have anywhere else to stay, and I don't want to drag my parrot back out in this weather," she said stiffly.

"Same here with Demon," Byron said firmly.

Sighing wearily, China asked, "Can't you go to your father's?"

"No, not now." His brow furrowed in thought. "Tell you what, why don't we make the best of it tonight."

"I really would prefer to leave, Byron," Marlene said coldly.

16

"You and your—your co-owner can work this out some other time."

"I'm afraid that's impossible," he replied, speaking in a low, soothing voice to the woman. "The storm is too bad, and it's difficult to find the way out of here in the dark." He glanced at the big mantel clock ticking away over the fireplace. "It's after midnight now. Let's all get some sleep and we'll work this out tomorrow."

China looked uncertain, and Byron said irritably, "Don't worry, Miss Castleberry, you're perfectly safe here with us. We're not into anything bizarre." His penetrating glance told her that she clearly wasn't his type, and China glared at him, feeling terribly annoyed.

She didn't like the setup, but she felt that she had little choice. She wasn't going out in the rain and wind, and anyway, she honestly didn't have anywhere else to go. Motels weren't that easy to find in that area. And she knew that the Davises had been asleep for hours. Besides, they never answered their door this late at night. A robber had taught them that lesson.

China appraised the couple again; they were both well groomed, and what little clothing they wore was quality, but what could one tell by such things? They were strangers. Still, there was the storm raging outside in the black of night. She didn't know when or if the police would come out on such a matter, and she didn't even know where they would come from. She guessed that this isolated area was handled by the sheriff's office, but in all the time her grandparents had lived here, she didn't recall them ever needing to call a law-enforcement agency.

China sighed. "I suppose you're right. We'll just have to wait until morning to get to the bottom of this mess." She rose and began to walk toward the master bedroom. When Byron called her name, she glanced back over her shoulder.

"Not that one," he said sternly. "It's already occupied."

China wondered how she could have possibly forgotten, but she retorted sharply, "I could see that. Do you mind if I get my bird out of there? Or do you want him, too? After all, he also belonged to Granny."

17

For the first time Byron laughed. "No, I don't want your bird. By all means, get him."

"And could you take your cat into the room with you and shut the door?" China asked stiffly. "I don't want him attacking my bird again."

Byron's smile was teasing. "I'm sure you'll lock your door, Miss Castleberry. But I'll take my cat."

"Thank you," she retorted icily. Then she opened the door, grabbed Blue's cage, and marched down the hall to the next bedroom. Once she was inside, she remembered that she had forgotten her luggage.

She sighed tiredly, wondering what she was doing here with these strangers. How had this happened? How had both she and Byron inherited the house? Or had they? She didn't know the man and he could be lying, but he had certainly known something about her and Granny, and he did know the lawyer's name.

Abruptly she pulled the door open and marched back into the living room. She paused only briefly when she saw that Byron and Marlene were still on the couch. Marlene's whispered words were not loud enough to be heard, and Byron was responding in a deep, low voice. China wished she hadn't walked back in. Now that she had, she had no choice but to pick up her luggage. Her fingers were already around the handle of the suitcase when Byron spoke, his voice husky.

"The other bedroom is down the hall."

"I know where the bedroom is," China retorted. "I'm picking up my luggage. You don't mind, do you?"

"Not at all. I was just trying to be helpful. I know you don't get up here often," he drawled. "I assumed you'd lost your way."

China wondered what he meant by that remark, but she wouldn't give him the satisfaction of a reply. Her suitcase in hand, she strode back to the bedroom to change into her nightclothes.

Her heart paused when she opened her luggage. It was still packed for her honeymoon in Europe. She had tossed a few pairs of jeans and a couple of shirts in on top of her beautiful

18

new clothes, but honeymoon garments were still neatly packed beneath. Even her passport was stowed in the suitcase.

China began to pull out the garments she had so carefully selected for her new life with Dereck, and she couldn't keep the tears from her eyes as she hung her clothes in the pine-scented closet on wooden hangers. Then she gently unfolded the lavish gowns she had chosen for her nights with her new husband. They were gorgeous, the best the shops carried, and worth a small fortune.

Well, Dereck wasn't here to see them, but she would wear them for herself. She selected a golden-colored waltz-length garment, and when she had slipped it over her head, she stood for a moment gazing at it in the old mirror over the bureau. She looked lovely, but that fact didn't alter her disposition one little bit. As quickly as she could, she climbed under the covers and turned off the light.

For a long time she lay in the darkness, fuming, recalling Byron's attitude. She couldn't get to sleep, and she frowned when she heard voices in the hall. Then she heard the door to the bedroom next to hers opening, then closing minutes later. She wished Granny had put the bedrooms on separate sides of the hall, but the library and the kitchen occupied the other side.

China was suddenly alert to every sound, imagining that she could hear the man and woman slipping into bed together and snuggling close. Her imagination was so vivid that she saw a very physical image of the two of them: Byron, blond and muscular, and Marlene with her sexy body and seductive red hair. The thought disturbed her, and she didn't know why she should feel that way.

Flinging the covers aside, China slipped her feet into her gold slippers, pulled on the robe that matched her gown, and walked out of the room and down the hall to the kitchen. She would have some hot chocolate. She had left some food in the cupboards when she was here before, and she remembered packages of chocolate so complete that all one had to do was pour in boiling water.

She pushed the swinging door open, then stopped abruptly. Byron was leaning against the counter, waiting for a pot of water to boil on the old stove. China hesitated, then decided she

19

would come back after he had gone, but as she turned away she heard him say her name.

"China." The word was soft and taunting.

She glanced back at him, regarding him warily, seeing him caught in the light spilling from the overhead lamp, his pale hair golden, his features like a Greek god.

"Don't run off," he drawled. "I won't bite you."

"I'm not running off," she said coolly. "I thought you might want your privacy." She could have added that she wasn't too sure he wouldn't bite, but she refrained.

Byron studied her pretty features for a moment, then deliberately let his gaze rove over her expensive robe and gown. Someone had obviously lavished large amounts of time and money on her—she apparently wore only the best, even to bed, alone, in an isolated cabin. He could just imagine how spoiled and impossible she was, and it irked him.

"All dressed up and nowhere to go?" he drawled sarcastically.

"I can think of a few places for you to go," China flung at him, "and before I lower myself to your level by telling you exactly where, I'll leave." Spinning on one of her elegant gold heels, she turned away.

Byron was taken aback for only a moment, then smiled lazily. Something about her appealed to him, although he didn't know why. He had already made up his mind about her.

"Come on back in here. You probably couldn't sleep and wanted a cup of hot chocolate, didn't you?"

It annoyed her that he seemed to read her mind so well. She walked back toward him and was acutely aware of his masculinity. He held the door open for her, and when her body brushed his as she moved past him, she felt a little thrill race over her skin. She really *didn't* like blond men, she reminded herself; it was just the late hour and the situation that had her behaving so strangely with him.

But she was determined not to let him see her discomfort. "I did want a cup of chocolate, in fact, Mr. Scott," she told him.

"Oh, come, now," he murmured, pinning her with those gray eyes. "Aren't we past the Mr. and Miss stage? It's Byron."

"Byron," she amended, thinking how well the name suited him. Arrogant. Haughty. Self-assured.

"I'm just heating up coffee water. There's only instant, but I was sure you were the chocolate-drinking kind."

"You're not sure of anything about me," she said, facing him. "You don't know me."

"No?" he asked idly. Then he poured boiling water into a cup and stirred it. China was surprised at how black the brew was. She would be up all night if she had coffee that strong before retiring.

She busied herself with a package of chocolate, pouring it into a cup, then turned back to the stove. Byron reached for the pot of water and poured it for her. "Thank you," she said formally. She was much too aware of the man, and she quickly took her cup and a spoon and walked over to the round pine table and sat down.

Following closely, Byron sat across from her. "Let's see," he said, "you're twenty-four, engaged to a young man who keeps changing his mind . . ." He gazed evenly at her to see the impact of his words. He had a preconceived idea of her despite her grandmother's almost worshipful love for her—in fact, because of it. The girl could have made more of an effort to see the old woman. It had probably never occurred to her or her parents to move Colleen off this isolated stretch of ground to where she could have some friends and interests. That would have inconvenienced them too much.

Byron wondered what kind of man China was engaged to. No doubt he had been attracted to her physically, then found himself in the position of waiting for her to grow up. She was a pretty thing in her way, but definitely not wife material, Byron was sure. It would cost some man an arm and a leg just to dress her in those gowns, if they were any indication of her taste in clothing. And catering to her whims would be a full-time job.

China stared at him incredulously. She didn't have to ask who had told him about Dereck; only Granny could have. It took her a moment to regain her composure. "It seems you have me at a disadvantage, Byron," she said, looking down at her cup as she stirred the contents. When she met his eyes, hers were veiled. "How well did you know my granny?"

"I ran errands for her from the time I was sixteen and old enough to drive. I knew her rather well."

Obviously, China wanted to say. "Why haven't I ever seen you here or heard her speak of you, then?" she asked, studying him thoughtfully. *Had* she ever heard of him?

"Summers we spent abroad," he said casually, and China found herself thinking that his family must be very well-to-do.

"I see," she murmured. "But it's strange she never mentioned your name."

"I'm disappointed," he said half teasingly. "She talked about you often. I guess she wasn't as fond of me as I thought."

"Apparently she was," China retorted, "if she left you this house, as you seem to think."

"She did leave it to me," he said smoothly. "I have a letter to prove it."

"So do I," she said dryly, trying not to show her anger. How could this have happened? Surely the lawyer knew that he had notified both of them about the will.

"So how long were you my granny's dedicated servant?" China quipped, wondering how old he was.

"I was never anyone's servant," he said firmly, his slate eyes meeting hers levelly. "I helped your grandmother because I felt sorry for her. She was vulnerable and she had no family here, only the old Davises to help her."

"How noble," China said, feeling an unwarranted surge of guilt. She and her parents had tried desperately to get Granny to come live with them after Gramps had died, but she had refused to give up her home. She had been stubborn when she wanted to be, and there had been nothing they could do about it.

Her parents both worked, as did she. And the trips were almost impossible with their irregular hours. She usually never had two days off in a row, since the stores were open six days a week. That virtually ruled out frequent trips. Even if they had been able to convince Granny to fly, getting transportation to and from the nearest airport would have been a problem, since Granny had never learned to drive.

Her thoughts returned to the man before her, whom she guessed to be about thirty years old. Surely her grandmother would have mentioned him if he had been as devoted as he implied.

"You really shouldn't have taken so much on yourself," she said. "Granny managed quite well with the Davises. She was a very self-reliant lady when she wanted to be."

"Did you know her at all?" he asked in an accusing tone. "She was a lonely old romantic who thought all people should live as compatibly as she and Gene had done. She used to worry that I would never marry," he remarked with a smile that heightened his good looks. "She seemed to think that I would be a playboy forever."

China had known that Granny was a romantic, but she had never known that she was lonely. She was surprised that this man thought so. Yet, he seemed to know a lot about her.

"You and Marlene aren't married, are you?" Actually it was the first time it had occurred to her that they might be. Instinctively she had suspected that they weren't; Byron had given different last names and hadn't introduced the woman as his wife, but that didn't prove anything in today's society.

Byron unabashedly shook his head. "I don't believe in marriage."

"I see." It wasn't the first time she had heard a man say that. Dereck had claimed the same thing when he started dating her. Anger caused her stomach to tighten in knots as she recalled how eagerly she had accepted his marriage proposal; oh, how she wished she had listened and believed when he had said that he would never marry!

Foolishly she had thought she had been the one to change his mind about matrimony. Even when he had come to her and asked her the first time to postpone the wedding only days before the event, she had still believed that he wanted to marry her. She had been acutely disappointed, but she had tried to be levelheaded about it. If Dereck needed time, she had reasoned, then they would simply have to give him time. But emotionally she had been quite devastated to think that he didn't want to marry her on the scheduled date.

She could feel the color leave her face. Maybe she wasn't giving herself enough credit, she thought bitterly. Dereck *had* wanted to marry her; he just hadn't wanted to give up the other

23

woman in his life. Closing her eyes, China tried to shut out that last memory of Dereck pleading with her to believe that the other woman hadn't meant anything, that he still wanted to marry *her*.

It had amazed her that he could even think she would consider it, having discovered his infidelity. She only wished that she hadn't wasted three years of her life with him. She had known he was a ladies' man, but she had never suspected, never even imagined, that he was seeing another woman. Other *women,* she corrected, for now she was sure that the one she had caught him with hadn't been the first.

But all that was over now, she reminded herself firmly, feeling the tears burn behind her lids. Dereck had gone from her life as though he had never been such an integral, intimate part of it, as though she hadn't built her entire world around him.

She had told herself over and over that the man she had thought she was engaged to was a fraud anyway. That cheating, lying person wasn't the man she had planned to spend her life with. She hadn't known him at all. She couldn't have really loved a man who would take her in his arms after he had gone to bed with another woman. She *couldn't* have.

"Falling asleep, China?" Byron asked in a deep voice.

China opened her eyes and glanced at him. "No, but I am tired. It's been a trying week for me."

"Fiancé change his mind again?" Byron asked perceptively, and China wanted to throw her chocolate into his face. Instead she took a sip.

"I changed mine," she said coolly. It wasn't a lie; she had called off the wedding—this time. She looked down at her cup, staring at its contents so that Byron couldn't see the distress written in her eyes.

"What do you do for a living?" he asked, smoothly changing the subject, much to China's relief.

"I manage two dress shops in Palm Springs. You seem to know so much that I thought Granny would have told you."

She was really quite proud of her job. She knew a lot about fashion, having once studied dress design. Ultimately she had decided that she liked working with people better than with pen and paper. She was compensated well for her ability to stay on

24

top of the latest fashions, ordering clothing that appealed to the elite of Palm Springs and dressing the rich in the most flattering styles and colors.

The wealthy owners of the two shops she managed valued highly her expertise and her ability to endure comments and complaints that would rankle Saint Peter. She had complete control of the shops, and she had enjoyed the challenge of making them prosper; but it had been like having her own business, and it required many additional hours she hadn't initially anticipated.

Dress shops, Byron thought to himself. Didn't that figure? A clotheshorse—a little girl playing at working. "It seems that she didn't tell me everything. And to manage two! I'm impressed. But how can you take time away now?"

"I have very good help. I know I can rely on them as long as I'm not gone for too long. I don't intend to be."

He watched her thoughtfully, then nodded. "Well, tomorrow we'll get this mess straightened out—and one of us will be gone."

His blunt words reminded her all too well why they were both sitting at this table. She found herself thinking that surely he wouldn't take this house from her if the matter was in dispute. She was the legal relative, but then, he had said that didn't count, hadn't he?

"If Granny talked about me, as you said, then you don't really believe she left this house to you, do you?" she asked.

"Stranger things have happened. Some people leave property to the mailman or the neighbor next door. They often feel strangers are more deserving than relatives."

China's dark eyes glowed brightly at the implication. She really wasn't in the mood to argue with this man tonight, especially when she was sure this whole thing would be resolved in the morning. "What do you do, Byron?" she asked, determined to change the subject as adeptly as he had.

"I own a chain of restaurants in southern California."

"Don't they need you there now?" she asked, saucily repeating his question.

He shook his head and mimicked, "I have very good help."

"But you don't need my granny's house, do you?" she asked

frankly. "I mean, financially you could buy any house you wanted in this area, couldn't you?"

He stared at her levelly. "I could buy most, I suppose. But I want this one, and it *was* left to me."

Again his bluntness shocked her. He *would* take her house if he could. The fact angered her more than she could say. He clearly didn't understand her attachment to this place, nor did he want to.

"Good night," she said, standing up abruptly. She turned on her heel and marched away.

She heard Byron softly taunt, "Good night. Sleep well in *my* house."

CHAPTER TWO

After a restless night China rose and wrapped herself in her robe. The house was quite chilly this morning. She went down the long hall and adjusted the thermostat, turning it up a few degrees, glad her father had been able to talk Granny into central heating.

She hadn't forgotten that she was sharing the house with strangers; in fact, she had thought of it half the night. She simply couldn't understand what this was all about. Granny wouldn't leave the house to a stranger: China knew she wouldn't have done that. So why had this man received the letter? Surely it was a mistake; but then, he clearly had known the old woman.

She glared at the closed door as she went past, and she wanted more than anything to pound on it suddenly and startle the two occupants sleeping so comfortably, as though they had the right to carry on their affair here in her grandmother's house.

26

"Lord," she said again, shaking her head, "I'm glad Granny's not here to see this. She wouldn't believe it." Still muttering to herself, she returned to the guest bedroom and uncovered Blue. Immediately he began to squawk boisterously, fluffing out his wings, paying his tribute to a new day.

"Shh," China rebuked, suddenly realizing that she really didn't want the strangers to awaken. When they were asleep, at least she could *pretend* to be alone. She didn't want to see any more of them than she had to. But the parrot, a creature of habit, had a mind of his own. It was morning, and he wanted to greet the new day as he always had.

"Thanks a lot," he said, repeating his favorite phrase as China walked down the hall with his cage in hand. "Thanks a lot."

"Shh," she cautioned again, hurrying to get him to the kitchen. But Blue was in rare form. He seemed to know that he was back in his old home, and he was all wound up.

At the top of his shrill voice Blue raucously announced, "Here I am. Where's the party?"

"It's right there in Granny's bedroom," China muttered sourly, "but I don't think you want to participate. Now, will you be quiet?"

She hurried toward the kitchen, but paused briefly when she glanced into the living room and saw Byron lying on the couch! Surely he hadn't slept *there*. Seeing him stir and not wanting him to see her, she rushed on to her destination. But she wasn't fast enough to escape him. She heard his voice just as she pushed against the swinging door leading into the room.

"China."

Pretending not to hear, she slipped into the kitchen. The door hadn't even stopped its swinging movement when Byron entered behind her.

"Now, what did you do that for?" he asked, folding his arms over his well-defined chest as he gazed at her.

Although China didn't intend to, she stared at his hairy chest; he was naked above the waist, and the pajama bottoms he wore rode down low on his lean hips, exposing the crisp curl of blond hair that wound its way down his muscled belly and

27

lower. She was horrified to find her gaze traveling down the line of hair until it disappeared.

"Thanks a lot," Blue sang out, and his shrill cry brought China back to the matter at hand.

She looked up into Byron's sleepy, seductive eyes. There were shadows under them, and his blond curls were tousled and disorderly. He looked as if he hadn't gotten much sleep. *Had* he slept on the couch all night? Perhaps he and Marlene had quarreled. She impatiently suppressed her thoughts; she didn't care where he had slept or what he had done.

"Do what?" she asked, at last responding to his question.

"Why did you encourage that bird to wake everybody in the house?"

"I didn't," she replied. "As you just heard, he speaks without prompting. He has a mind of his own."

"So does my cat," Byron commented.

"What's that supposed to mean?" she asked, recalling all too vividly how the cat had attacked the cage the night before.

"It means you woke him up and he wants out."

"I've no doubt about that," she muttered. "I'm surprised he's not striped. Probably like you, he has the morals of an alley cat."

"What did you say?" Byron asked, his eyes glittering.

"I said, Well, that's just too bad. As you stated last night, you and Marlene have rights because you arrived first. Blue and I got up first, so your cat can just stay in Granny's room with your girl friend."

"She's just a friend," he replied easily, a mocking smile on his beautifully formed lips. "What's makes you think she's my girl friend?"

China wanted to say that she had seen how close a friend the woman was, but she found her gaze being drawn to his mouth. His lips formed a Cupid's bow; she had never found that attractive in a man before, preferring instead thinner, more stern lips. But Byron's looked firm and full, and kissably appealing. She glanced away. What was it about this man that sent her blood pressure spiraling—besides his wanting to steal her house? She told herself that if she had met him under any other circumstances . . . But she brushed away the thought.

28

If she had met him under any other circumstances, she wouldn't have given him the time of day. She didn't like his attitude, and anyway, Dereck was the man on her mind. The two years she had been engaged to him couldn't be wiped away so easily. *My God,* she told herself, *two years!* She couldn't imagine Byron being engaged to anyone for that long. He looked like an impatient man, one who would carry out his plans in a hurry when he made them. But then, he had said he wasn't the marrying kind either, so he wouldn't have married, hurry or not.

"You're thinking stupid thoughts again," she muttered aloud, her mumbling such a habit that she wasn't even aware of it.

Some of the customers in the two dress shops she managed had driven her to it. Rich ladies with money to burn and time on their hands, they would come into the shops and try on dress after dress, hour after hour, then waltz out empty-handed, only to return later and demand *their* dress, which had oftentimes already been purchased by someone else.

Suggesting that they have her hold a dress they were particularly interested in always proved futile. China had resorted to muttering to herself the moment they were out of earshot as a matter of self-preservation. It was either that or bite her tongue, and muttering was less painful.

"Not only are you talking to yourself, but you didn't answer my question," Byron drawled.

She glanced at him again, seeing all too well that he was barely dressed. He was barefoot too. Something about barefoot men had always seemed very sensual to her. Not that she had a foot fetish, she thought to herself, but most men were very careful to keep their shoes on at almost all times. Her gaze returned to his face, and she saw that he was smiling oddly at her.

"What was your question?" she asked, honestly having forgotten.

"I asked what made you think Marlene was my girl friend?"

"Well, for crying out loud," she snapped, "I saw you with her on the couch. What on earth am I supposed to think? That she's your sister?"

Tossing back his head, Byron laughed. "No, I certainly hope not. I told you last night, I'm not into anything bizarre."

"Frankly," she replied dryly, "you seem a bit bizarre to me."

Byron chuckled. "Really? What makes you say that?"

Shrugging off his question, China opened Blue's cage and took him on her finger. He made a soft clucking noise, and she kissed him. "Kiss," she cooed gently.

"Kiss," he repeated in a soft, buzzing tone, and then he make a kissing sound with his tongue.

"Charming, absolutely charming," Byron said mockingly.

China looked at him rebelliously, and he glanced first at her, then at the bird.

"What's the matter with that damn thing?" he asked.

"Nothing," China replied defensively, following his gaze.

"Why are his feathers gone from his beak to his eye?"

China shrugged. "No reason."

"I'm not a bird expert, but you'd better see someone who is," Byron commented. "That bird has a problem. Instead of kissing him, you'd better get him some medical treatment."

Glancing at him with her dark eyes, China replied, "I've already had him treated. His feathers are growing back in."

"Why did they fall out?" he asked, curiously assessing the brilliantly colored parrot.

China had to concede that Blue did look odd with his feathers gone on one side of his face. "He's sexually frustrated."

For a moment Byron stared blindly at her, then he laughed uproariously.

"I hardly find it amusing," China said coolly.

Shaking his blond head, Byron commented. "Damn, I don't either. It's just that I didn't ever expect to meet a sexually frustrated parrot. Are you sure someone isn't pulling your leg? Or did you self-diagnose—I mean, for the bird," he added tauntingly.

"Highly amusing," she retorted. "I took him to a bird specialist. It's not that uncommon. He needs a mate."

"Don't we all?" Byron murmured, a little under his breath. Then he said, "Why don't you get him one?"

"I inherited the bird from Granny, who hadn't had him long and didn't know much about him. She felt sorry for him, so she took him in when someone wanted to get rid of him. It's not a simple matter of just finding a mate for him. He has to be surgically examined to see which sex he is, then a compatible blue-fronted Amazon has to be found."

"Why do you refer to him as a male if you don't know what sex he really is?" Byron asked, his eyes teasing her.

"He needed to be designated some gender, and since I don't know which he is, male is as good as female."

"Do you really believe that?"

"This conversation is ridiculous," China declared.

"I'm really interested," he insisted, but China had her doubts. "I don't know why you haven't already found a mate for that parrot."

"I told you, it's not that simple."

"Have a heart, lady," Byron teased. "That boy's in trouble—if he is a boy."

"Don't you have something else to do besides talk about my parrot?" China demanded, irritated by his comments.

He nodded. "Yes, in a little while I'm going into Monterey to talk about your house, which I believe to be mine. Do you want to drive with me, or do you prefer to go in on your own? I believe we'll get more accomplished if we do this thing together and get it over with."

"Fine," she said sharply. She couldn't believe he really wanted *her* house—him, with his chain of restaurants. Well, she would see just what the situation was when they reached the lawyer's. Until then, there was little point in speculating or harping on it.

"I'll be ready in half an hour," she said. "We can go in my car."

"That little thing," he commented. "I saw it from the window. I would be too cramped. Why not my Rolls?"

"Why not?" she repeated sarcastically. "That will be fine, but my car is perfectly comfortable."

"For you, perhaps," he said. "But I'm six feet two inches tall."

"I'm five nine," she returned, "and I have plenty of head room."

"I've never liked tall women," he commented. He really

31

never had; he usually found them too overconfident as a whole, too aggressive. He believed the theory that tall people, be they male or female, were blessed with certain advantages; there was the feeling of power that came from height. He had been exposed to those facts in college psychology, and he had seen them substantiated too many times to ignore them.

He had seen many gorgeous, feminine women who were over six feet tall; in fact, he had hired a few to manage his restaurants, confident that they would be capable of dealing with any of his male employees who felt superior to the female species. But oddly enough, he liked his women small. He didn't want to go into the psychology of that; he just liked them that way. Perhaps it was the chauvinist in him.

China looked at him sharply; she had surmised that he liked small women when she had seen how short Marlene was—not over five feet two inches, she was sure—but she wondered if he had deliberately made that crack intending to insult her. "That makes us even," she said coolly. "I've never liked blond men. I prefer mine dark and masculine."

He smiled dryly. "Oh? Is your elusive fiancé dark?"

"That's none of your business."

Byron laughed. "I'm not dark, but take my word for it, China, I'm masculine."

"I'll take your word for it," she retorted. "I sure don't intend to find out any other way."

To her chagrin he laughed again. "Why did they name you China—a tall, willowy thing like you? I think of China as fragile and fine, like porcelain."

"I wasn't born this tall," she said sarcastically. "As a baby, I was really quite tiny—six pounds, I believe. And because I had very pale skin and very dark hair and was so small, my mother was reminded of fine china."

"She was at least partly right," he said, his gaze holding hers for a moment before he scanned her face brazenly. "You have lovely coloring."

China glanced away. First an insult, then a compliment. She didn't need this man's confused observations.

"Why do you like small women?" she flung at him. "Do they make you feel superior—you and your big-man strength, and those helpless little females?" As soon as she had asked the question, she felt like biting her tongue. She was furious with herself for caring that he had said he didn't like tall women. She didn't care what he liked. All she wanted was to get him out of this house, whatever that took.

"Where did you get a key to this house?" she demanded suddenly, not giving him a chance to reply to her first question. "I know the Davises didn't let you in. They were expecting me, and I have my own key."

"So do I. I have had for several years."

"I don't believe it!" she insisted. "Granny would have mentioned it. She would have mentioned you."

He moved his broad shoulders in a casual gesture that attracted her gaze. "Believe what you want."

"I've never seen you before," she said accusingly. "Where were you when Granny was buried? You weren't at the funeral."

"I was en route here when I was involved in a car accident. I was hospitalized for three days." He turned away from her. "Marlene will be getting up. I don't want to fight with her for the bathroom, so I'm going to get my shower—unless, of course, you want in there first. There is only one bath, you know."

"Of course I know." She glanced away from him. "You go ahead."

"Want to save water?" he asked, looking back at her over his shoulder.

"What do you mean?"

"If you want to save water, you can shower with me. I'll let you," he said, grinning tauntingly at her. "That way we can save on the utilities."

"Thanks a lot, but don't do me any favors. Ask Marlene. Maybe she's that desperate."

"That's a good idea," he replied. Then he laughed as he went out the swinging door. China could still hear his laughter as he went back down the hall.

"Thanks a lot," Blue repeated.

"Oh, shut up, will you?" she growled at him, taking out on the bird her anger toward Byron.

33

"Oh, shut up," Blue mimicked, and China shook her fist at him.

After walking over to the cupboard, she opened it to see if there was anything she could have for breakfast. She was taken aback when she saw that it was fully stocked, all the shelves bulging with canned and packaged goods. Byron, of course. He had really come here ready to take over, she told herself, pursing her lips in anger.

She turned to the old refrigerator and opened it. Yes, as she had thought, it, too, was filled to capacity. "Why not?" she muttered. Then she took out a couple of eggs and poured herself a glass of milk. She briefly wondered if she should wait for breakfast until Marlene and Byron came out, but she decided against it.

When she had scrambled the eggs, she fixed herself a plate, adding a piece of toast. Then she took Blue on her shoulder and her glass in hand and went over to the round pine table and sat down.

The kitchen had a view of the ocean through its broad windows, and while China ate, she stared out at the churning water, thinking how much she enjoyed being in this house. Blue occasionally demanded a bite of food, and China hand-fed him bits of egg and bread and let him drink milk from her glass.

As soon as she was finished, she put the plate and glass in the sink and quickly washed them. Then she put Blue back in his cage and returned him to the guest room. She would have to leave him, of course, while she went to the law office, but she intended to see that Byron locked his cat in another room.

She waited until she was sure the bathroom was free, then went in to take her bath. She had run water and was just settling down in the tub when the door opened.

"Oh, I beg your pardon," Byron said in response to her surprised gasp. "I didn't know you were in here."

"Well, now you do, so get out," China ordered, trying futilely to hide her long, slender body with a single washcloth.

"I'm in no hurry," Byron drawled, his frank gaze roving over her, warming China as it swept from her breasts, inadequately protected by one hand, down her smooth belly to the washcloth she held between her long, silken thighs.

34

"Damn you!" she flung at him. "I've had enough of you. Get out of here. I don't even know you, but I'm really beginning to dislike you."

Making no move to leave, he smiled lazily at her. "That's funny. I don't know you, either, but I'm beginning to like you better." His liquid-silver eyes whipped over her once more. "Better all the time." Then he closed the door.

China had just released her breath in a ragged sigh when the door opened abruptly. "And, China, you haven't had me at all —not yet," Byron said with a husky laugh. Then he shut the door again.

China could feel the color flood throughout her body. For a man who didn't like tall women, he certainly had done a thorough job of visually examining every inch of her. She shook her head, hating herself for feeling what she was feeling.

She had been flattered by Byron's appraisal; her act of outrage had been surprise, and anger, at finding him here. But she had been flattered, all right. She didn't know what her problem was since she had met him. She wasn't man-crazy by any stretch of the imagination. And she really *didn't* like blond men. Besides, she had just broken up with Dereck.

She sank down farther into the water. Hopefully today Byron would get out of her life. She certainly wouldn't have any other occasion to see him again. He lived in Santa Monica and she lived in Palm Springs. If he and she were in this area, they would be thirty miles apart: she would be here and he in Monterey, at his father's.

Swiftly, China took the washcloth in hand and began to scrub her body. But no matter how fiercely she raked the cloth over her pale skin, she couldn't wash away the sight of Byron standing there, staring at her nude curves. And every time she thought of it, she felt warm all over. He was having the strangest effect on her; she honestly didn't understand it. Maybe it was because of her rage at Dereck, but that was hardly an excuse. She couldn't forget that Byron was here with that redhaired sexpot! Making love to her right in Granny's house!

Furious all over again, she finished her bath, dried off, and pulled her robe back on. When she had returned to her room, she dressed in one of the nicest outfits she had brought with her, a shimmering silver-and-gold silk dress that clung attractively to her tall figure and outlined her assets to best advantage.

She didn't miss the fact that this particular outfit was incongruous with the ranch; it had been purchased in anticipation of a lovely dinner in Europe, but it made her feel so attractive. The color was very flattering, and she left her dark hair long, the waves glistening blue-black against the richness of the dress. Then she slipped three-inch silver-and-gold-striped open-toed heels onto her narrow feet.

Her makeup was done to perfection, and she was very pleased with herself as she spoke soothingly to Blue and left the room, her beige coat slung over her arm. Byron and Marlene had apparently finished breakfast; they were waiting for her in the living room, and her gaze traveled over them in alarm. Byron was dressed in jeans and a dark blue sweater, his outfit molding perfectly to his long, lean body. He was wearing loafers on his feet.

Marlene, dressed similarly, displayed ample cleavage, her V-neck navy sweater hugging her full breasts, her blue jeans outlining her curvaceous hips. She looked at China curiously, but she didn't comment. Still, the look made China feel terribly overdressed.

"You look lovely," Byron commented as his penetrating eyes assessed her openly. "But it is pouring rain outside."

His second statement effectively diminished his first, clearly implying that she had to be out of her mind to dress like that for such weather. "I don't intend to go for a walk," she replied, forcing a smile. "I assume you're going dressed like that, so why don't we get under way?"

Giving her a lazy smile, Byron stood up. "Fine." He turned back to Marlene. "We won't be too long, I'm sure." China looked away when he squeezed the redhead's hand.

Of course there was no reason why he shouldn't, China told herself, but she felt so damned awkward standing there that she turned on her heel and began to walk toward the door. At least Marlene wasn't going to see the lawyer with them.

Somehow Byron reached the door before China did. He smiled at her provocatively, then opened the door, and she rushed out into the rain, pulling her coat on en route. It was still pouring, the day almost as dismal and dark as the night had been.

"Wait here and I'll get the car," Byron instructed. China wanted to tell him not to do her any favors, but she wasn't that foolish. She would be soaked if she walked with him around the side of the house to the garage.

"Thanks," she said only half sincerely. Byron had rubbed her the wrong way right from the start, and she was in this strange situation because of him. She didn't feel like being charming now.

She wasn't at all surprised when he pulled up in a silver-gray Rolls-Royce fit for a king. She had seen the women arrive in such cars at the exclusive shops she managed, their chauffeurs patiently waiting for them while they shopped for hours on end for a single dress for a particular occasion.

"Well, dammit, get in," Byron yelled, and China realized that he had opened the door for her while she was standing there, daydreaming.

"Sorry," she murmured. She eased inside and he leaned across her to shut the door. He put his arm across her chest, and she was sure he let it linger there longer than necessary.

"No problem," he said, looking at her thoughtfully.

Both of them seemed disinclined to make conversation during the thirty-odd minutes it took to drive to the lawyer's office in Monterey, and as China sat looking out her window, she wondered what Byron was thinking. Every once in a while she was sure she felt him watching her, but she didn't look at him. Instead she stared blindly at the passing scenery, not seeing the drenched fields and remote homes that dotted the road leading to the city.

When Byron finally pulled into the driveway of an office building, China drew her attention back to the matter at hand. This had to be some kind of mistake; she just knew it. She didn't have any idea what she was doing with this stranger, but she wanted to get this over with.

The receptionist recognized Byron, and China uncomfortably noted that she would again be at a disadvantage, for she had never met the lawyer.

"You don't have an appointment, do you?" the round little woman asked.

Byron shook his head. "No, but somehow I think Lloyd may be expecting us."

"I'll ring," the woman said. She said a few words to the lawyer, then nodded to Byron. "He's with another client now, but he'll see you in just a short while. Why don't you sit down?"

China noticed the woman's curious looks as she walked over to the nearest couch, but she didn't give any indication of the interest she had created. Sitting down, she crossed her long legs, then picked up a magazine, thumbing through it as casually as if part of her future weren't hanging in the balance, dependent upon what the lawyer said to her.

She could feel Byron watching her, but she didn't raise her eyes. He didn't sit down, and she had the distinct impression that he was lounging against the wall, simply staring at her. She didn't dare look up, and she hoped no one could see how her fingers trembled as she turned the pages of the magazine, neither seeing nor reading its contents.

At last a man walked out of the office, bid the receptionist good-bye, then left. Another man came out, an older, balding man with a broad smile and a warm face. China looked up to see him shaking Byron's hand.

"Come on in, Byron," he said warmly. He glanced over at China. "No," he said, "it can't be." Then he grinned. "I'll bet you're Colleen's little granddaughter."

"Not so little," Byron corrected, watching as China stood up, rising to her full height of six feet in her tall heels, "but she's the one." He looked back at the older man. "Now, tell us, Lloyd, what the hell's going on here? Who inherited the house?"

Waving at him impatiently, Lloyd held out his hand to China. "Come on over here, honey. Let's all go into the office."

As she walked toward him, her movements graceful and fluid, she smiled. Tall she might be, but she carried her height well, using it as the asset it could be.

"She's a beauty, isn't she, Byron?" Lloyd asked, glancing at the other man.

"If you like that type," Byron said wryly, and China felt like kicking him.

Instead she smiled warmly at Lloyd. "Thank you, Mr. Thomas. It's a pleasure to meet you."

"Please call me Lloyd. I feel like I know you. You don't look a bit like Colleen, except that she, like you, was a beauty, especially when she was younger. Tiny but lovely." He winked at her. "No wonder Gene kept her stuck out there on that old ranch. She was a real eye-catcher."

China smiled as he ushered her into the office and seated her in front of his desk.

"Well, don't stand there all day," he said to Byron. "Sit down."

Byron did so, saying impatiently, "Let's get to the heart of the matter, Lloyd. Now you know what this is about. You sent me a letter saying I'd inherited the Castleberry house. China insists that you sent her one too." He looked at her as if he didn't believe it. "As granddaughter, she feels she's the rightful heir. I can understand that, but apparently Colleen wished to disinherit her, for whatever reason—neglect in her old age, I suspect."

Lloyd shook his head, speaking before China could make a sharp retort.

"No, no, not at all, Byron. Colleen loved China dearly."

"Then did you make a mistake sending me the letter?"

"Of course not. I'm quite competent, even if I am getting old."

"What are you saying, then?" China asked.

"That you both inherited the house," Lloyd said with a smile. "That's how Colleen wanted it. You own the house together."

CHAPTER THREE

"You can't be serious," China sputtered. "She must have been confused when she wrote up a new will." She glared at Byron accusingly. "Or did you manage to somehow trick an old lady into doing this?"

"No, no," Lloyd hastened to assure her. "I'm sure neither of those things is true. She was perfectly sane. She and I discussed this. She was very pleased about it. I gathered that you and Byron were friends and knew about this arrangement, although Colleen insisted that I not put it in the letters I mailed to you."

Byron suddenly broke into laughter, shaking his head as though at a joke no one else was aware of. "Well, I'll be damned. I'll bet that little old lady was trying to play matchmaker, right up to the end. She kept telling me she wanted me to meet her granddaughter, and I kept procrastinating."

China didn't find it at all amusing; matchmaking or not, she couldn't imagine what had made Granny do this to her. The woman had known how China felt about the cabin, how special it was to her. And to give half of it to this stranger . . . !

"Well, she certainly never told me she wanted *me* to meet *you,* and I don't know if this will is valid. We might just see what the courts think about it." China's dark eyes were blazing. She wouldn't share her special place with this man, who had no respect at all for it. He could have any house he wanted anywhere. This one meant nothing at all to him. It was her birthright; it was all she wanted. And she meant to have it!

"Oh, it's perfectly valid," Lloyd assured her hurriedly. "I have it all right down here. The house is to be equally inherited by both China Castleberry and Byron Scott, Jr."

"Junior?" China questioned, making a connection in her

mind. "Junior? You're *the* Junior who's been helping Granny over the years?"

Byron nodded. "Yes, she did call me Junior to distinguish me from my father, who was Gene's friend and a frequent guest at the house."

Now it was China's turn to break into laughter. "Granny did talk to me about you, but I thought you were some skinny, gangling teen-age boy who hung around the house to help with the errands. I never knew—I never thought—You're Junior! I just can't believe it." Her husky laughter filled the office, and Lloyd began to laugh with her, albeit a little nervously. Only Byron kept quiet.

"I'm sorry," China said, recovering her composure. "I can't tell you the times Granny bemoaned the fact that I hadn't yet met Junior."

"Nor I Che-Che," Byron said, effectively putting her in her place. "It seems that we were in the same boat, both avoiding what we thought would be unpleasant—and not without some measure of truth, I now find."

His statement sobered her, and China turned to Lloyd. "I would like to buy out Byron's half of the house. Can I do that?"

Her job enabled her to keep a generous sum in her savings account. She earned a good living and she had been frugal, residing in a comfortable but modest apartment while she saved money for the house she and Dereck had planned to share eventually. Now that she didn't need the money for that purpose, she could apply it to the cabin.

"Yes, of course, but only if he's willing to sell," Lloyd murmured, seeing that they weren't the happy twosome he had expected.

"I'm not," Byron said bluntly.

"But what possible use can you have for the house?" China cried, turning to him with pleading eyes. "It was my grandparents' home, my father's home. It has sentimental value for me."

"Oh, I have a use for it," Byron said, smiling a little sardonically. China wondered just what he meant, but she wasn't about to ask him.

"The house actually means something to me," she said coolly.

41

"And to me," Byron insisted. It really wasn't that important to him, but he wasn't going to give in to this woman so easily. Colleen had had a purpose in leaving the house to both of them, and he wanted to be sure that it was only a romantic whim of an old lady before he gave his half back to China—if that was what he decided to do. At the moment he wasn't so sure. He *did* want to get to know her better—a lot better.

Lloyd was beginning to look very uncomfortable. "I do hope you two can work out some equitable agreement. I'm sure Colleen didn't anticipate this when she wrote her will. She was so happy about it. I assumed—Well, I don't know what to say." He reached into his desk and produced some papers. "While you're here, please sign these. That's all I can do for you now, and I do have another client scheduled."

There was nothing to do but sign and leave. China was irritated with herself for having come with Byron at all. The last thing she wanted to do was get back in his car. She felt cheated and betrayed because Granny had known what the house meant to her. She didn't understand how Granny could do this to her. Her parents would be shocked to learn about this, to think that Granny had wanted to leave her house to China *and* this man in the hope of bringing them together. It was demeaning and deplorable. China's lips tightened into a thin line. Maybe Mother wouldn't be as shocked as she thought.

Her mother had always thought Dereck was wrong for China. But in spite of that, she had gone ahead with the lavish and time-consuming arrangements for a big wedding. Everything had been done: The minister had been arranged for; the church, the cake, and the reception had been taken care of; the announcements had been sent out. And, right along with China, her poor mother had to face friends and relatives to tell them the wedding was off—a second time. Only this time it had been China's decision.

Still, she told herself, Granny *must* have been losing touch with reality if she had really gone to this extreme to get a man for her granddaughter. And yet, even as she thought it, she knew it wasn't true. Granny had remained alert and active right up to the end. Mercifully she had died peacefully in her sleep.

In fact, China reluctantly conceded that this was just the

kind of thing Granny would have gotten a real kick out of. The old woman had had a terrific sense of humor, and she had enjoyed a joke on herself as well as on someone else. If she had done this, it wasn't just because of a blatant desire to find China a man but out of sheer enjoyment of the complexity of human relationships.

If Granny had known this man at all, she would have known that he and China would clash in all kinds of ways. China, who refused to tumble into bed with a succession of men; Byron, who obviously saw all women as objects for his own pleasure. Byron, who had confessed that he didn't like tall, outspoken women; China, whom Granny certainly knew, preferred dark men. Neither of them had been the least bit interested in Granny's less-than-subtle attempts to introduce them.

A grudging smile tugged at China's full lips. She had heard of arranged meetings, but this one took the cake. How Granny must have planned and schemed to organize this before she died.

She had always known that her grandmother was strong-willed, a woman not to be denied but who would keep right on trying to match her granddaughter up with a man, even after death. . . .

"Shall we?" Byron said, smiling at China as he stood up. She had the distinct impression that he was enjoying this tremendously, and she detested him for it. It was absurd: He didn't need her house. And he didn't deserve it!

"Do I have a choice?"

He shrugged. "We all have choices, but it's time to go. The man said he's busy."

"I heard."

When he tried to take her arm in his, China moved away from him. "Good day, Lloyd. I have a feeling we'll be doing business together again."

He nodded. "I'll enjoy that." But China noticed his discomfort.

After Byron shook the other man's hand, he and China walked out the door.

"Well, *Junior*," she said sarcastically, "what now? Shall we

43

cut the house down the middle and separate it, or will you eventually be reasonable and sell me your half?"

"I couldn't do that," he murmured. "I couldn't possibly disappoint your Granny."

"Oh, come, now," she snapped as they walked outside in the pouring rain. "You're doing this out of spite. What do you want with that house way out in the middle of nowhere?"

"Why, China," he said in a teasing voice, "a cozy, secluded place like that—the possibilities are limitless."

"I'm sure you can find some other place that suits your— your *needs* just as well as that one!"

"But I want that one. It suits me just fine."

"Let's not play games," she flung at him, her dark eyes brooding and angry. "I love that house. I spent a lot of time there when I was growing up. It means nothing to you. What will it cost me to buy you out?"

"More than you could ever afford," he said swiftly, and China could feel her heart sink.

"Why? Why are you doing this?"

"That particular house appeals to me. In fact, it's recently become even more attractive."

"Oh, damn you," she muttered crossly. "You rich people think you can treat other people any old way. You're not being fair."

"All's fair in love and war," he commented.

"We don't need to label this, do we?"

Byron suddenly smiled. "I don't. Do you?"

She looked at him oddly, wondering at his teasing smile. "I don't know about you, but for me it's war, and I don't intend to stop with things the way they are. How can we possibly share the house? It's ridiculous."

"China," he said very seriously, his steady gray eyes holding her dark ones, "don't waste your time and money trying to fight me. I've made up my mind. I have money to throw away. Unless you do, don't attempt to harass me legally. It won't work."

"Don't lay down the law to me," China retorted. "I'm not impressed by your money. For all you know, I can afford to fight you—and I will if I make up my mind to!"

44

For a moment Byron seemed surprised by her spirit. Finally he told her, "I'll go get the car."

China stared out into the pouring rain as he crossed the parking lot. "Damn you," she muttered softly. "You hateful playboy tycoon!" He was going to keep half of her house, and what would she do about it? It did seem to be quite cut and dried legally. It reminded her of two people being awarded custody of a child. How did they work it? He got it two weekends each month and two weeks during the summer, and she got it the rest of the time? "Damn," she muttered again, then climbed into the car as Byron swung the door open for her.

"I have two weeks off now," she said coolly when she had settled in and he had started the car. "You, obviously, can take off whenever you want. Will you please take your girl and go? I'd like this time to myself."

"China, you shock me," he teased. "How greedy of you! We share the house equally. I, too, have two weeks off now. I can't come and go at the drop of a hat any more than you." He looked over at her, his slate eyes twinkling. "Why can't the three of us spend the two weeks together? After all, we're already here."

"There are five of us," she said in an icy voice, not at all appreciating his sense of humor. "I don't believe in blended families. My child doesn't get along with yours—or your woman."

Byron broke into hardy laughter. "What you meant to say is that there are three predators and two innocents in that cabin and that it won't work."

"It won't work," she responded emphatically, "not because we're separated into innocents and predators, but because I do not want you and your—*friends* there."

"All right," he said unexpectedly, shocking China into silence. "Marlene and I will go to San Francisco"—she looked at him hopefully, thinking this was too easy, too good to be true—"on one condition."

"That figures," she muttered. "What is it?"

"That you keep Demon."

"No!" she cried. "I let Blue fly free. His wings aren't clipped. Your cat will kill him."

45

"Hmm," Byron said, considering the fact, "that could be a problem. I guess I'll have to take him with me."

China almost couldn't believe her good fortune. He was suddenly too agreeable. "That would certainly be best." She looked at him suspiciously, wondering what he would say next.

"All right," he said. "We'll give you a little breathing room, let you have the house to yourself for a while."

Swallowing feelings of triumph, China said, "Thank you, Byron. I appreciate this." She had expected him to remain obstinate right to the bitter end, and she had envisioned having to share the house with two strangers and a cat—on what should have been her honeymoon. This was working out after all, and for the first time she felt she could let her guard down a little.

"I don't know what we're going to do in the future," she said, still finding their joint ownership unbelievable, "but I guess we'll work something out."

He smiled, his gray eyes glowing warmly. "Oh, yes. We'll work something out. I'm sure of it."

Again China looked at him warily. The statement was reasonable enough, but the way he had said it bothered her. "Oh, stop it," she muttered, barely under her breath. The man was being generous, considering that he apparently had as much legal right to the house as she did.

"What did you say?"

She tossed a smile his way. "I said thanks."

"That's what I thought you said," he replied, but he was grinning at her knowingly.

The rain was still pouring down, making the landscape around them forlorn and dismal, but suddenly China's spirits lifted. She and Blue would have the freedom of the house. They would get to spend the thirteen days they had left without being bothered by a single soul.

And oh, how she needed this time. Just the thought of being at home in her apartment, accessible to her friends with their well-meaning comments, sent a shiver up her spine. She didn't want to face her painful memories of love gone wrong at the moment. She would still get the comments, she knew, once she returned, but by then she would at least have pat responses.

Sighing audibly, she stared blindly out at the falling rain. She and Dereck had planned to honeymoon in Europe these last two weeks in October, sampling the sights and the fabulous cuisine. Now she and Blue would sit in the cabin, and she'd eat sandwiches and frozen dinners and drink Cokes.

She had bought the most gorgeous gowns in the two stores—at considerable expense, even with her employee discount—in anticipation of her nights with Dereck. Now Blue would be nibbling at the lace and biting holes in the exquisite fabric. The thought of her sharing her honeymoon with a sexually frustrated parrot actually made her smile in spite of her anger and hurt over Dereck's behavior.

But the smile was brief. Damn Dereck! How could he have cheated on her? And why had he pleaded with her to set another wedding date after they had canceled the one set for Valentine's Day last year? Why hadn't he been honest and told her he was seeing someone else and that that was the reason he wasn't ready for marriage?

China's teeth closed down on her lower lip and she bit into it painfully, remembering how carefully she had worded her notes the first time she told those on her guest list that the wedding had to be canceled. And then again last week! Oh, God, she didn't want to think about it anymore. She couldn't keep going over and over it.

She realized that she was glad it was finally over. For weeks she had been afraid Dereck would back out, despite his assurances that he loved her. But once burned, twice shy, and her insecurities had been valid.

Three days before the wedding, she had stopped by Dereck's apartment and found him there with a woman. Three days before the wedding! She knew she was fortunate that it had been before instead of after they were married, but the hurt had been no less. It had been such a total shock that her face still flamed at the memory. Well, she had learned her lesson.

"China."

Glancing over at Byron, she forced a smile. How could she have forgotten that he was with her?

"I like you better when you're muttering to yourself," he commented lightly. "At least I can guess at what you're thinking then." He rubbed his chin, and China's gaze was drawn to

47

the strong line. "Let's see, now you're sorry you agreed to let me go away."

"No, no, of course not," she insisted quickly.

"Well, what else was I to think? There you were, staring vacantly, looking miserable. That's how it usually is when I leave women." He was laughing lightly, but China wasn't amused.

"I'm sure it is," she retorted. "Unfortunately that's how it is when a lot of men of your type leave a woman."

"Did your man leave you, China?" Byron asked, his tone serious.

"He did not! I told you I called off the wedding this time."

Suddenly, Byron inexplicably felt bad for her. He sensed the deep pain beneath her sharp reply. There were two sides to every story, weren't there? Maybe the guy was at fault. Byron was beginning to suspect that Colleen Castleberry had some basis for loving her granddaughter. He was starting to see that this was a vulnerable, soft woman in spite of her sharp tongue. Maybe she had had some kind of viable reason for not seeing her aged grandmother often, although he didn't know what it would have been. It was a long trip for him, too, but he always managed it several times a year.

He nodded, but his eyes were solemn. "When was the wedding to have been?"

China bit down on her lip again. "Today," she said quietly, but her voice was tear-choked. "Today we were getting married and tomorrow we were leaving for the British Isles."

"Have you ever been to Scotland?"

China shook her head. "No, but I'm eager to go. I've talked to people who have been there, and they say it's absolutely beautiful. It's my favorite place to read about. It's full of legends and mysteries and romantic history."

Byron smiled. "Yes, you would love it. I have relatives there, so I've been there several times. It is enchanting."

China fell silent again. Big Sur was going to be her Scotland, and that was that. She still had both tickets for the trip, but they had been canceled, of course. Someday she would go, when she could enjoy it without painful memories.

They weren't far from the house, and China was amazed at

how easily Byron found it, weaving in among the tall trees and hills, until she remembered that he had come many times to help Granny. *Junior,* she told herself, the thought bringing a smile to her lips. This handsome blond was Junior.

Byron parked the car on the graveled drive beside China's so that he and Marlene could more easily reload their suitcases, and China hurried to the front door. Byron was right behind her, and both of them were wet by the time he opened the door and they went inside.

China felt an unreasonable surge of jealousy when she saw Marlene curled up on the old couch near the fireplace, stroking Demon, the redheaded woman looking as sultry and exotic as the purring black cat. The two of them made a dramatic picture, and mentally China included the blond and handsome Byron with them.

She found herself walking over to the hall coatrack to hang up her wet coat. "Damn," she muttered sourly. She didn't know what it was about the two of them that got to her so badly.

She actually envied Marlene, and she certainly didn't know why. What good did a man like Byron do a girl? He sounded just like Dereck. He had already said he didn't believe in marriage, but then, maybe Marlene didn't either. It wasn't the ultimate fantasy for some women. China sighed. Granny had instilled the wrong ideas in her granddaughter's head; she had led a little girl to believe that one man could and would love her forever.

China turned back to the couple. "Well, I'll leave you two to pack," she said brightly.

Then she spun on her heel and moved away, going to the guest bedroom to retrieve Blue. She could hear Marlene's pleased response as Byron talked with her. When she walked into the room, she found Blue clucking and muttering to himself, making buzzing sounds. He looked at her with his gold eyes, and he began to call out, "Kiss. Kiss."

China opened the door and took him on her finger, then she talked to him and rubbed his chest. She couldn't wait until Byron and Marlene were gone and she would have the house to

49

herself. She realized that she had been uptight from the moment she entered and found this unexpected development.

To her surprise, in almost no time there was a knock on her door. "Come in," she called.

Byron stepped into the room. "We'll be leaving now," he said, looking from her to the bird.

It was precisely what China wanted, but now that the occasion was at hand, she realized there were things they needed to discuss. "What will we do about this house?" she asked. "I mean, how will I know when you'll be here and when I should come? And what about the legalities of owning it jointly? How will I get in touch with you? And I had wanted to make a few changes in the decor, bring up some of my personal things."

Byron smiled. "Aren't you really saying you want to see me again?"

"No, *Junior,* I'm not!" she said fiercely. "I wish I never had to see you again, but I won't have a choice if we both turn up here like this."

He nodded. "I see. Well, I'll be in touch. Perhaps I'll stop back by on my way home."

"When?" she asked, her heart suddenly beating in alarm.

He shrugged carelessly. "I'm not sure, but what does it matter? You're not going anywhere, are you?"

"Well, I don't know. I may go into town or something like that."

"Then I'll wait for you."

She didn't intend to argue with him, but the thought of him coming back disturbed her. She wanted to be completely alone. She wished they could do this by phone or mail.

"Why don't you just leave your card?" she asked. Abruptly she set Blue on the top of the cage and reached for her purse. "Here," she said, pulling out one of her own cards. "You can call me later and we'll talk this out."

He took it and slid it into his shirt pocket. "I'll put it here, next to my heart," he said teasingly, and before China could step away, he grabbed her wrist, drawing her to him. As he looked down into her dark eyes she was momentarily mesmerized by his penetrating gaze. He pulled her to him, his gray eyes still holding hers. When she opened her mouth to protest, her

50

full lips trembling nervously, Byron lowered his head and his mouth closed down over hers possessively.

China wanted to respond with outrage to his bold caress, but his mouth moved against hers provocatively, stirring some primitive response inside her. She could feel the fire begin to burn in her veins, and Byron's heady sexuality fired her blood.

His lips moved hotly against hers, making her heart beat erratically. He was holding her so close that she couldn't pull away, and for a single insane moment she didn't want to. His body was long and lean and muscled, and with her heels on she stood almost as tall as he. She could feel the excitement of him, from his mouth all the way down to where his thighs pressed against hers, and he was very exciting indeed.

At last she had the good sense to twist away from him, wiping at her lips with her fingertips. She had meant to brush his kiss away, but her fingers lingered where her mouth still throbbed from contact with his. His gaze was drawn there, and China quickly lowered her hand.

Abruptly, China slapped his face. "You don't need a cabin," she accused angrily, her own weakness in submitting to his kiss causing her to overreact. "What you need is a brothel! You have one heck of a nerve," she muttered. "You with your woman right here in the house with you while you kiss me."

For a moment Byron's gray eyes filled with storm clouds. Then he smiled mockingly. "Oh, my, Che-Che, perhaps Granny was right. Maybe we should have gotten together," he murmured, his voice thick.

"I seriously doubt that!" she retorted, and she couldn't help but wonder how he would behave with a mistress if Marlene were only a good friend.

Before she could think of an appropriate response, Byron laughed softly. "I'll be going now, China, but I'll be in touch."

Riveted to the spot where she stood, China stared after him. She told herself that she should go and at least say a few words to Marlene, but she didn't feel like being hypocritical. There were several more words she would like to say to Byron, but she wouldn't waste her time. She simply wanted these people out of her life. She stayed right where she was until she heard the door close and the car engine finally start. Then she realized that she was trembling.

She went into the front room and stood there, hidden behind a lacy curtain, staring out at the silver Rolls until it disappeared down the rutted road. Then she went over to the fireplace and put more wood on the fire. Suddenly she was very cold.

Would she ever see Byron Scott again? And did she want to? The question disturbed her deeply. She was attracted to him in a way she didn't understand. She could still feel his lips, warm and possessive against hers. His kind of man was even more dangerous than Dereck's. Byron made no pretense of establishing a long-term relationship with a woman. He had said he wouldn't marry, and China doubted seriously if one woman could ever hold him.

"My God," she muttered aloud. Why was she even indulging those absurd thoughts? It was ludicrous! She didn't care; she had no intention of becoming involved with him. Dereck had done enough damage to her heart and pride to last a lifetime. She would never make that mistake again; she had had enough of the Derecks and the Byrons of the world.

CHAPTER FOUR

Surprisingly, China found herself at loose ends all that afternoon. Everywhere she walked in the five-room house, she saw the image of Byron's face. A faint hint of his after-shave lingered in the air, and she recalled how heady the scent had been when he kissed her. She reminded herself that she didn't care for the man at all, but she couldn't deny how easily he had awakened her passion.

In all the times Dereck had kissed her, she didn't ever remember being swept away as completely as she had been by that single kiss of Byron's. She told herself that Byron had been able to stir her senses so easily because of the intense emotional upheaval she was experiencing. But was that true? Suddenly she realized that she wanted to believe that Marlene was only a friend, as Byron had said, but she had seen them with her own eyes.

"Will you stop behaving like such a damned fool," she told herself aloud. Then she made herself stop thinking of the man. Blue had gone to sleep with the coming of evening, and China roamed around the house, trying to keep from thinking about Byron.

The house was still filled with many of the personal effects of Colleen Castleberry. There were dainty little doilies covering the Victorian tables and chair arms, adding a feminine touch to the rough-wood cabin. The couch had pillows Granny had made herself and embroidered with delicate, brightly colored patterns of flowers from the woods she had loved. And paintings of the forest birds and animals filled the walls of all the rooms. Granny had done those, too, sometimes with Gramps's help. The sight of the possessions Granny had loved only served to make China miss the old woman more, and she went back to the living room.

"Granny, I love you, wherever you are," she said aloud. "I wish you were here."

The rains continued to come down, beating against the windows and roof. Ordinarily, China loved the rain, but today it made her feel confined and forlorn. The weather was much too bad for her to walk out in the woods, and she was beginning to feel like a prisoner when Karly Davis came over late that afternoon with a tray in her hand.

"Good evening," China said cheerfully, opening the door wide for the woman, who was bundled up against the wind and rain. "Come on in."

She lifted the heavy plastic and cloth covering the tray to peek at the food. "What have you got there? It smells wonderful."

"It's homemade soup and cornbread," Karly said, her bright eyes twinkling proudly. She was in her sixties, but her figure was slim and erect, and she walked spryly. She glanced around the room suspiciously, and China surmised that she had seen Byron.

"Come into the kitchen with me and have a cup of coffee," China said.

Seeming eager for company, Karly followed willingly. China knew the questions would· come eventually, and she waited, watching as Karly removed the steaming bowl of soup and bread from the tray and sat down in one of the big pine chairs.

"So, what's been going on over here?" the old woman asked at last. "Seems like I saw young Byron Scott, Jr., coming and going—and with a red-haired gal."

China smiled to herself. That red-haired gal was hard to miss. But then, so was Byron. "Yes, he was here." She filled the teapot full of water and set it on a burner to heat. Then she walked over to the table. "Karly, did you have any idea that Byron would inherit this house with me?"

To China's surprise Karly lowered her eyes and stared down at her hands. "Yes, I suppose I did know a little something about that."

"Why didn't you tell me?" China asked, leaning closer. "I almost died of fright when I came in here and found those two. I'd never met him, and I didn't know that he was the Junior whom Granny had talked about."

When Karly looked up, China was shocked to see the mischievous gleam in her green eyes. "He's a handsome boy, isn't he? Colleen thought you and him would make such a fine pair."

"Karly, I was engaged to another man. What did Granny hope to accomplish by complicating my life with this one?" Her grandmother's matchmaking attempts had been ridiculous and humiliating; she didn't need anyone to find a man for her. She was perfectly capable of making her own decisions.

"Shucks, honey," Karly said sheepishly, "nobody ever expected you to marry that young man of yours—not really. A man and a woman don't need to be engaged for two years, not if they're really planning to marry." China could see that the other woman was embarrassed when their eyes met. "Your young man didn't have marrying on his mind as much as he should have."

China could feel her face burn as a hundred thoughts tumbled wildly in her mind. No, Dereck hadn't given his full attention to their marriage plans. He had been too busy thinking about other women. In fact, she was amazed that he had bothered to propose to her at all.

In view of the circumstances, why hadn't he just asked her to move in with him instead? But then, what would he have done with her *and* his other women?

The question left a bitter taste in her mouth, and she turned her attention back to Karly. "I wish you had told me that Byron was here when I phoned. I wouldn't have come."

"I didn't know he was coming; and anyway," she said, again lowering her eyes, "you took me so by surprise. I'd been told you would be honeymooning. I didn't know what to say when you said you were on your way up."

China nodded. She hadn't known what to say herself; she hadn't wanted to explain that her marriage was off again. Just the thought sent her blood pressure spiraling.

Smiling faintly, China murmured, "Of course it wasn't your place to tell me about him. Granny," she muttered softly, shaking her fist at no one in particular but looking heavenward.

"She meant well, China. She was so sweet on Junior and so sure that the two of you would hit it off if you could only meet. She figured that it would be unavoidable if you both owned the house. Besides, Colleen looked on him like a grandson. He was real good to her."

Now that she had seen him, to hear someone actually call Byron "Junior" almost made China laugh. How that tall, handsome, virile, sophisticated hunk of a man could have gotten a nickname like Junior was beyond her. She was surprised and disturbed by the string of adjectives she had applied to him so thoughtlessly, and she did not want to consider why.

China turned back to Karly. "I know Granny appreciated him," she said, remembering Byron's own words.

"It was true. He's a fine young boy."

A fine young boy, China thought to herself. *That thirty-one-year-old man?* And anyway, as far as she could see, his appeal was mostly physical. He was just another womanizer, a playboy type like Dereck, she thought bitterly. In his way, maybe he was even worse than Dereck. *No* woman would be safe with

Byron. Hadn't he charmed Granny unbelievably? It was almost criminal, the way he had succeeded in getting half of the cabin.

Karly's eyes took on a reminiscent look. "Why, I remember one time when Byron was a bit younger and he was trying to break one of Gene's horses for him," she said, smiling. "He had decided all by himself that both Gene and Randolph were too old to do it, and he climbed up on that horse like he was a pro."

The woman paused to shake her head at the memory. "The boy had never been on a horse that wasn't broken, and he got the surprise of his life. He tried real hard to hang on, but that horse bucked him off like he was a fly. He landed right on his rear."

China laughed. "I wish I had seen that."

"Well, that wasn't the half of it," Karly continued. "He wouldn't give up. No, sir. He got right back on, and I'll be durned if he didn't finally break that stallion. But for the rest of his visit, Colleen had him sitting on a pillow. We all tried not to laugh, but it wasn't easy. Cocky thing, he was, but he was a fine boy."

China found herself smiling. She should have guessed that Byron wouldn't have given up. The teapot whistled, signaling that the water was ready, and China was grateful for something to do. She went over to the counter and prepared two cups of instant coffee.

"Eat your soup before it gets cold," Karly urged when China returned, and the younger woman obeyed, eager to have something substantial. All day long she had munched on crackers and cheese.

Karly changed the subject to local gossip, people China knew nothing about, and she listened with interest, glad for something to distract her from her own problems. The time with Karly passed quickly, for once the old woman got wound up, she only needed a good listener, and China had been glad to be that.

At last Karly stood up and went back into the hall to get her coat. "I'd better be getting back before it gets dark and Randolph begins to worry about me in this rain. It's going to get worse, I hear, before it gets better. The radio man said there's a new storm brewing on the coast, so you be prepared. If you get scared or if you want anything at all, you come on down, you hear?"

"Thanks, Karly. I'll wash the dishes and bring them over tomorrow."

"No you won't. I'll just take them on back now and do them at home."

China saw that it would be useless to argue, and she thanked Karly and walked with her to the back door, which opened out to a path leading down to the small house. The wind lashed at the door savagely, tugging it so that China had to cling to it. Rain was thrown up on the weathered porch as though by the bucketful.

"Will you be all right going back to your place?" China asked worriedly. The woman was old, and China was concerned for her safety. A fall could be dangerous to anyone, and especially an older person.

"I'll be just fine. I'll walk careful. You know, I used to come up here and see Colleen twice a day, sometimes more. Of course, at night Randolph would usually come with me, but he's laid up today with some virus or something. He's been feeling bad for the last couple of days. When the storm lets up, I think I'll take him into Monterey to the doctor." She held up the tray. "I made the soup for him, but I thought you would want some."

"It was delicious, but you shouldn't have left Randolph to come over here. Is there anything I can do for him? Perhaps you could call his doctor at home. I'd be happy to drive into Monterey to get a prescription or anything else you might need."

Shaking her head, Karly said, "Thank you, no. We're used to doing for ourselves. It's much too bad for any of us to go out in this weather. I'll let you know if he gets worse. Now, you take care."

China wrapped her arms around her body and stood there on the porch, shivering, as she watched Karly walk down the steps. She had to resist the urge to hold the old woman's arm. She knew Karly wouldn't appreciate her solicitous nature. As she had said, they were used to doing for themselves. Granny had been like that—or so China had thought. Apparently, Byron had done more for Granny than she or her parents had suspected.

The back-porch light lit Karly's path for only part of the way, and when it flickered momentarily, China had to restrain herself from running out after the woman to make sure she got home. She was a lot more used to walking that path than China, and finally China went back inside. Although she tried to resist the urge, she did go over to the phone a few minutes later and call to make sure Karly had arrived safely.

As the hours wore on, the storm did worsen. China put more wood on the living-room fire and turned up the central heat a few degrees. She didn't especially like stormy weather, and the old cabin creaked and groaned under the fierce battering. Twice she thought she heard someone at the front door, but it was just the old brass-ring door knocker being rattled by the wind. It banged against the wood with such force that China was almost convinced a person was doing it. The windows shook and the tree branches danced against them eerily. All in all, it was rather spooky.

Finally, China turned on the ancient radio, muttering, "Might as well hear how bad this thing is going to be." That was part of it, but the other part was that she was becoming unsettled and wanted the sound of another human voice.

She knew nothing could happen to her. The house was secure and it had survived its share of storms in its time. It was just that the weather was so confining. China had intended to remain here for two weeks, but she had thought she would be able to get out in the woods and walk off some of her disappointment and anger at her newest failed plans.

" 'The best-laid plans,' et cetera," she muttered to herself as she fiddled with the radio, trying to get a decent station. She heard more crackles and static than anything, but finally she located a station with some music—no news—quickly finding that the music had a soothing effect on her nerves. She turned up the volume to drown out the violent sounds of wind and rain.

Walking over to the front window, she stared out at the blackness before her. She was grateful just to know that Karly and Randolph were down at the little house, and she wished desperately that Granny were alive and here with her. Granny hadn't been afraid of anything. She had come to this area as a bride of sixteen, and she had lived in this same house for the rest of her life. There had been additions and renovations to it from time to time, but it had been her home for sixty-one years.

China turned away from the window with a sigh. Granny and Gramps had been married for over sixty years, and it had been a good marriage. Her own parents had been married for thirty. She smiled grimly to herself. She knew that those statistics were rare in a time when divorce was more the norm than not, but she wondered if she would ever marry at all. Some people were opting not to, but she had tried darned hard to give it a go herself.

She thought of the beautiful satin-and-lace wedding gown that had been left hanging on the back of her bedroom door. She had purchased it almost a year before, for the first wedding date, which had been in February. She had lovingly gotten it out of storage last week. The memory depressed her, and she flipped off the radio and went back to the guest room to change into her nightclothes. She didn't bother to switch rooms even though Byron and Marlene had left.

Tonight she selected a daring deep-red gown for sleep. It was a splendid piece of nightwear, with the bodice cut into a deep *V* and the long sleeves and floor-length hem edged in darker red lace. The fabric was soft and clinging, and it hugged her curves.

She took the matching red robe off the hanger. It wasn't much of a covering, since it too had the deep *V*, and it was held together by only a single ribbon around her waist, but it was beautiful. She felt quite elegant and lovely in the gorgeous clothes, for her sleepwear usually consisted of a short nightie, or a flannel gown in cool weather. It wouldn't take long to get used to this kind of luxury, she told herself with a little smile.

Then she recalled Byron's words: *all dressed up and nowhere to go.* All dressed up and no one to see, no one to care. Well, she was doing this for *herself,* she reminded herself firmly. Abruptly she slid her feet into the red high-heeled slippers that had come with the outfit and strode into the living room, causing the hem of the garments to swish around her ankles, her anger in no way

59

detracting from the beauty of her long, slender body in the clinging outfit.

She was still much too aware of the storm, and she turned the radio back on, hoping the music would soothe the savageness inside her. She took the paperback she had been reading and settled down on the old couch where she had first seen Byron and Marlene in each other's arms.

Suddenly she picked up one of the small round throw pillows, stood up, and beat the couch furiously with it, as though she could remove the memory of the blond man and the redheaded woman holding each other there on *her* couch. Soon she had worked herself into a fury, pounding wildly at the still-firm cushions, moving up and down until she had covered every inch of the couch.

It was wonderful therapy, and soon the ridiculousness of it caused her to break into deep laughter. But it had worked: It had released some of the tension and anger bottled up inside her. She replaced the pillow, then curled up on the couch with her book. It was a romance by her favorite author, and she gradually slipped into a good mood as she read about the conflicts of the couple involved and their loving triumph over obstacles.

Inexplicably she found herself remembering Byron's kiss and how it had excited her. She had been alarmed by her response; she really couldn't understand what had gotten into her. Why had Byron kissed her, anyway? To see if he could possibly be interested in Colleen's granddaughter? It was all absurd, and she didn't want to dwell on it.

There was a brightly colored crocheted coverlet folded over one of the chairs, and China pulled it off and covered herself with it. To her surprise she soon drifted into drowsy contentment. The storm still raged overhead, but the fire crackled comfortingly in contrast, and the coverlet warmed her. The last thought on her mind as she drifted into sleep was the final commitment the lovers in her book had made. She smiled and snuggled down deeper into the cushions of the couch.

Byron Scott was cursing bitterly when he finally had to stop his car at the end of the road leading to the Castleberry place.

The storm was raging and some of the roads had been washed out; there was no way he could get out of the area that night and maybe not the next day. A tree was down across the only road in and out of this secluded spot, and he had heard on the radio that a landslide had blocked the coastal route. He could take another freeway if he could get to it, but he wasn't going anywhere until morning. He couldn't even get his car off this road.

"Damn!" he muttered, shutting off the car's engine. The dirt road was a mass of mud and water, and he was stuck in it. He couldn't move farther, and neither could anyone who came behind him. But then, who would? he asked himself.

No one else would be that foolish. All day, there had been reports of the storm damage on the radio, but he hadn't listened —and he knew the area. No, he hadn't listened. He had taken Marlene to a female friend's house farther north, as she had requested so that she could continue her vacation, then he had turned right around and driven back down here.

He sat there in the car with the storm lashing out all around him, the rain tattooing the roof of his car like a continuous hail of bullets, and remembered that Marlene had told him she had sensed his interest in China.

He had denied it. But the truth was that he *was* interested. No matter how he kept telling himself that she wasn't his type, he kept seeing her as she had looked in the tub when he had opened the door. She was beautiful; there was no other description. And he kept remembering her there in the guest room that last time. He could still feel the way her soft lips had moved under the pressure of his. He hadn't meant to kiss her; he had had no intention at all of that then, but it had happened.

China's comment about Marlene being his girl friend kept coming to mind; she really wasn't his girl friend. In fact, this had been the first time she had gone away with him, and China had turned up to make the situation embarrassing and uncomfortable for all three of them. Byron had been as eager to leave as Marlene.

He ran his hands through his hair. He had wanted to rest as much as he had wanted anything. He had needed to. He had just opened a new restaurant in Los Angeles, and he was exhausted. Marlene had been tempted by the privacy and seclusion of the cabin too. She owned an exclusive Italian restaurant in Santa Monica, and she had wanted a chance to escape her responsibilities and problems for a while.

She was recently divorced and still smarting from that experience. She had been the one to suggest that she go with him to the cabin when he had told her where he was spending his vacation. Her mother had agreed to take care of her children for the two weeks so that Marlene could get away.

Byron shook his head as he thought of what a fiasco the vacation had turned into. He and Marlene had been friends for years, since she had opened her restaurant on the same block on which one of his was located. In fact, he often ate at Marlene's restaurant. He had, of course, known her husband.

It had crossed his mind that, with two weeks together, he and Marlene would make love in the cabin, but he hadn't planned it. Up until this time they had only been friends. He thought Marlene was a beauty, but he never became involved with married women. He had had plenty of women over the years to keep him occupied, many of whom Marlene had seen in her restaurant.

In fact, that had been a big part of the problem. When Marlene saw China walk into the room, she had immediately thought that she was one of his women.

He shook his head again, thinking of how Marlene had told him she had made a mistake; she shouldn't have come with him at all. She realized that she valued his friendship and his advice too much to become his lover, to put herself in the position of becoming one of the women in his life—and perhaps in his past. She had turned to him out of the loneliness of being newly divorced.

Marlene had insisted that she could tell he was attracted to China, and though Byron had refuted it—he wasn't insensitive and he was sure he hadn't paid China any attention in front of her—she had still felt that they were better off keeping the status quo.

Byron had agreed. He valued her friendship, too, and he had known that once they made love, their relationship would have to change. He didn't have many close friends, and Marlene was

62

one of them. He realized that he wanted to keep that precious closeness with her, and he had been relieved that she had been the one to bring up the subject. They had parted with the easy rapport of long-established friends, knowing that something just hadn't worked out.

"Damn," he growled again. So Marlene was in the plush comfort of her friend's home and he was stuck here on this muddy road to nowhere, wondering why. It was pitch black outside and the rain showed no signs of slowing, much less stopping. He had been glad that Marlene had been able to make other plans that pleased her; he had suggested that they go on up to San Francisco and do the town so that she could still make the most of her free time, but she had wanted the peace and quiet of a private home. She had hoped to drive up and see her friend anyway during the two weeks, so this had worked out all right for her.

Byron rubbed his chin idly, wondering why he hadn't had enough sense to check into a motel somewhere and enjoy his solitude. He had passed through Monterey, stopped by his father's house for a while, then started for home. Or was he lying to himself? Hadn't he really started for the Castleberry place, despite the lateness of the hour? Didn't he have a ready excuse for China about Marlene changing her plans and leaving him with some days to kill? Hadn't he already decided to tell her that he thought they might as well get the house situation straightened out? Hadn't he worked it all out in his mind?

Well, by damn, here he was. He rummaged around in the glove compartment until he found a small flashlight, then he buttoned up his jacket, cursed himself for not having his raincoat, and climbed out of the car. He didn't have a hat or boots, and he knew he would be drenched in no time. When he reached back into the car for Demon, the black cat reared up on all fours and hissed at him.

"I don't like this any better than you," Byron muttered, "but we don't have any choice. Now, come on before I leave you here." He reached for the cat and it darted into the backseat. In no mood for games, Byron opened the back door, then lunged at the animal. Demon, not to be outdone, jumped up on the back of the front seat, then plunged out the open door. When he felt the impact of both rain and mud, he realized his folly and yowled disconsolately.

"Serves you right," Byron griped, shining the light on the cat as he reached down to get him. Demon was already wet when Byron stuffed the protesting animal inside his jacket. He cursed again when Demon clung with sharp claws, his wet, muddy feet damp against Byron's shirt.

"Dammit, I ought to leave you in the car!" Byron snapped. Supporting the animal with his left arm held tightly to his body, he shut the car door and started up the rutted road. His loafers sank down in the mud and mire. "Hell," he said in disgust. It served him right being here.

He felt his way along the side of the car until he knew he was walking on the road, and then he began the treacherous trip toward the house. He knew it couldn't be far, but it was so damned dark that he couldn't tell how far. He had turned off the main road leading to this private one sometime back, so it really couldn't be any great distance.

It seemed like forever that he sloshed along in the muck and mire and the drenching downpour. His loafers were caked with mud, making the way even more precarious, and his feet were wet. Rain was plastering his hair to his head and pouring down his face, and Demon kept up a constant growling noise that made him want to make the cantankerous cat fend for himself. Finally he thought he saw the vague shape of the cabin in the darkness.

He quickened his steps, hurrying on the slippery road, muttering and cursing to himself, causing him to think of China and her constant conversations with herself. He hoped she had a fire going because he was sure he was going to catch his death of pneumonia. He hadn't even brought a change of clothes with him. He was lucky to get himself and Demon to the house, much less drag along something else. With his flashlight he found the way up the path to the front door, and he breathed a sigh of relief when he was at least somewhat sheltered from the rain.

Not wanting to frighten China by entering the house suddenly, Byron beat on the door with the old brass door knocker. He waited a moment, then rapped again, but he got no response. He wasn't going to stand out in the rain all night, even if he did have to startle China. Rummaging around in his pant pocket, he hunted for the key to the door.

Inside the house, China had been vaguely aware of the old door knocker rattling in the wind and the rain. It had made her uncomfortable, but she had investigated the sound several times already and had known that it was just the weather playing havoc with the ring. She turned restlessly in her sleep, listened for only a moment, then settled back down beneath the coverlet. The fire was dying now, and the room was growing quite dark. It was late, and she told herself that she should get up and go to bed, but she was too comfortable and too sleepy. She closed her eyes once more and drifted back to sleep.

Juggling the sulky cat with one hand and hunting for the key with the other was quite a trick, but Byron finally found what he was looking for. He sighed in relief when he inserted the key and opened the door. The faint glow of the fire was all that lit the house, and he stumbled over the rug in the entrance way as he stepped inside. Deciding that it was late and China must have gone to bed, he headed toward the table at the end of the couch to turn on the lamp.

China heard someone stumble in the darkened room and immediately all her senses went on alert. Alarm spread through her system like a wall of fire; she was barely out of her half-asleep state when the stranger appeared by her head, but instinctively she reached for the pitcher of flowers on the coffee table. As the shadowy form bent forward near her she grabbed up the pitcher and brought it down on the intruder's head. China heard the crash of the pitcher and felt water splash on her. Then the heavy weight of a body fell against her.

Frantically she flipped on the light. Nothing happened. She tried again, turning the tiny knob on and off, but there was no light to drive back the blackness and let her see who was there.

She could feel a man's inert form sinking down on top of her, and her terror increased. "Oh, dear God!" she wailed as she clutched at him. Suddenly a cat clawed its way up from the neck of the man's jacket with a wild shriek that startled China so badly that she screamed. Yellow eyes wide, the panicked cat stared at her briefly, as though hypnotized, then fled down across the stranger's chest.

China was still gasping in fright when she got a glimpse of the spooky dark form streaking out of the room, his wet blue-black coat momentarily reflecting the dancing blues and reds of the fire. The sight of the cat triggered something in her fright-paralyzed brain. A black cat and a man who could find his way around the room in the darkness.

"Oh, no!" she cried aloud. "Byron!" As the cat vanished she thought briefly of Blue, but her first concern was the stricken Byron lying partially on top of her. Holding him away from her as best she could, she eased out from under him. She managed to maneuver him so that he fell on the couch, then she got up, moving his legs quickly so that he was lying completely on the couch on his side.

After taking a deep breath, she rushed over to the mantel and lit the two lamps there, kept always at the ready for such contingencies. When she returned to Byron she was struck by the inane thought that she hadn't known such a virile man could look so pathetic. At first she told herself that it served him right for sneaking back here in the middle of the night, but as she stared at him, her unease began to intensify. Some of the flowers and pieces of pottery still clung to his blond head and neck, making him look so ridiculous that, in her panic, she didn't know whether to laugh or cry.

"Oh, Byron," she murmured aloud. "What have I done?"

He was hurt, but how badly? From her limited knowledge of medical emergencies she didn't know what to think, but she suspected that it was entirely possible that the blow to the back of his head had resulted in a concussion. A lamp in hand, she ran to the bathroom, grabbed up a towel, and dipped a wash-cloth in cold water. She recalled reading somewhere that one shouldn't attempt to treat wounds when a concussion was suspected; the proper procedure was to wait for medical help. But she wasn't going to get any medical help. She had to take charge of the situation and do what she hoped was best.

On her return trip she briefly stepped into the guest bedroom to make sure Demon hadn't found Blue, and when she saw no evidence of the terrified cat, she left the room, closing the door behind her. After going back to Byron, she placed the cold cloth on his head. He didn't move, and panic spun up inside China like a whirlwind. What if she had killed him? Oh, God, what then?

CHAPTER FIVE

China made herself calm down. It wouldn't do either of them any good if she panicked. She tried to find Byron's pulse but couldn't. He was soaked through and through. Rain—and the water from the pitcher of flowers—had apparently run down inside the collar of his jacket, and even his shirt was wet. His pants were sopping wet where the protection of the jacket had ended just below his waist. China knew she had to do something to help him.

She picked up the telephone to call the operator for help, but as she had suspected, the phone was dead too. Her next thought was Karly; the old woman was used to making do there in the back country, but she decided she couldn't call Karly out in the rain. Randolph was ill, too, and anyway, what could Karly do?

Quickly, China went over to the fire and tossed several more logs on it, building up the blaze so that it was high and hot. Then she returned to Byron. She examined his head, and when she saw the place where the wound was, her heart almost stopped. Mercifully it was bleeding very little. She felt his damp face and neck and finally located a pulse beating strongly. Thank heavens he was breathing!

He began to groan deeply, and when he reached up to touch his head, China grabbed his hand.

"Oh, thank God, you're all right!" she cried, but when he didn't respond, she wasn't so sure.

"Byron," she said, shaking him. "Byron, are you okay?"

He stared at her with dazed eyes, and she knew that he was still stunned. She had once gotten a little experience with this kind of thing when Randolph Davis was kicked by a horse. He hadn't had a concussion, but he had had the nearest thing to it. He had suffered severe headaches, and he had been confused and groggy, symptoms Byron was showing.

China forced herself to remember what they had done for Randolph. They had phoned a doctor, but by the time the doctor had arrived and examined him, they had been instructed only to watch him in case his condition worsened. Brow furrowed, she strained to recall what the course of action had been. It had been so long ago. She remembered that the doctor had kept questioning him and checking his pupils. And they had purposely kept Randolph awake for several hours.

China stared at the wounded man. "Do you know who you are?" she questioned. "Tell me who you are."

He seemed puzzled by the question, but when she prompted again, he managed to say his first name in a slurred voice.

"Do you know who *I* am?"

He stared at her, frowning heavily. "Sara?"

China shook her head and knew that he really was dazed. She also knew she had to get his wet clothes off and keep him warm. The very last thing she wanted to do was undress Byron Scott, but what choice had she?

"I have to get your clothes off," she said, as if she needed his permission. "Damn, what am I telling him for?" she muttered. "He won't be any help." But she sure wished he could do it himself.

It was a difficult task, to say the least. China found herself wishing that Byron were completely unconscious; he was groaning and trying to brush her hands away in his present state.

She finally managed to unbutton his coat with trembling fingers, but how to get the damp garment, which was clinging to his wet shirt, off those broad shoulders was a real problem.

Trying to hold his inert form up a little and still keep him from toppling to the floor, China tugged and struggled as gently as possible, so she didn't make his injury worse, until she had the coat off his shoulders. But then how was she to get it down his arms and out from under him? She frowned, glancing around the room as though looking for some miracle to make all this easier.

"Wouldn't you just know something like this would happen to me?" she muttered aloud. "Who else on earth would defend herself, then have to undress the intruder? Why is it always my luck?" She rolled her eyes heavenward, but there was nothing to do but get on with the task.

With considerable effort she got Byron up into a sitting position and succeeded in getting one of his arms free. Then she rolled him toward her and somehow managed to free the other arm and get the coat off him.

Next she tackled the shirt, leaving the pants for last, even though she had to unbuckle his belt to get his shirt hem out. She had to peel the drenched shirt away from his body by employing the same tactics she had used for the coat, but the shirt wasn't as difficult. She tried to work fast, but she wasn't used to undressing a semiconscious man, and despite herself, she couldn't help but admire this one's physique.

Oddly she almost felt as if she were taking advantage of him in his semiconscious state. "That's a laugh," she said aloud. "If I were the one in this predicament, he wouldn't have any qualms."

Pausing for a moment, she struggled to get up the courage to take off his pants. She gazed down at his muscular body, noting the contours of his broad chest and the thick body hair glistening damply in the firelight. He really was beautiful.

"You damned fool," she muttered. "Will you get on with it?"

She finally had the presence of mind to put the coverlet on the upper half of his wet body. When she unzipped his pants, Byron murmured something unintelligible and reached out for her breasts.

"Damn!" she cursed, brushing at his hands. Alert or not, this man instinctively knew what he wanted to do when a woman started to take his pants off. "Lie still, you maniac," China commanded sharply.

Muttering and cursing, she worked furiously to get his pants down his impossibly long, lean legs. She frowned as she fought with them, then realized that she would have to lift his hips up if she hoped to take his pants off.

For a moment she was stymied. She couldn't do that. But she drew in a steadying breath, rolled him a little away from her, and tugged until she had the pants down over his hips. She could feel her face flame when she saw the navy underwear outlining his virile body. They were hardly decent, so brief were they; she really didn't know why he bothered to wear anything at all. But she was glad he had, she reminded herself.

In her haste to undress him, she had forgotten to take off Byron's socks and shoes, and eventually she discovered that that was why she couldn't get his pants off. She stripped off his shoes and socks and finally got his pants all the way down his powerful calves in spite of the damp material clinging rebelliously. At last she succeeded in getting the wet pants over his feet. Then she flung them down on the floor, relieved that she was finished.

Looking at him again, China knew that she wasn't really finished. For a moment she hesitated; surely wet underwear wouldn't kill him.

"Oh, get on with it," she told herself. "You've come this far. Just hurry up and get it over with!"

She knew she had to be quick about this or not do it at all, so she began to slide the shorts down Byron's body. It was no easy thing to do, since, as she had done with the pants, she had to raise the man's hips.

She heard him murmuring something that sounded like "Hurry up, baby," and she grumbled aloud, "Do it yourself if you don't like the way I do it."

She was forced to move her hands partially under his hips, and she could feel the cold, hard flesh of his buttocks against her warm palms. Quickly she pulled at the damp shorts until they were down his thighs, and at last they were off him.

China let her breath free in a ragged sigh when her job was done. Reaching for the towel, she began to pat Byron dry, and against her will she found herself staring at his gorgeously detailed body. She could feel her face burn with embarrassment, but for a moment she simply couldn't stop. He was the most well-defined man she had ever even imagined seeing; it seemed unfair that one man should be so perfect in every way. He had said he was masculine. She certainly had no doubts about that now.

Finally she came out of her reverie and began to wrap him securely in the coverlet. Then she was able to give her attention to his head wound. She began to pick the pieces of gray pottery out of his thick, damp hair, and she tossed aside the red flower petals that clung tenaciously to the wet curls.

For a moment she wasn't sure what to do next; she wasn't very accomplished in the nursing department, but she didn't think she had done any serious damage. She had stunned him, that was easy enough to see, but he was breathing regularly.

She brushed away more flowers and pottery fragments, then tenderly dried his wet face and hair with the towel she had brought from the bathroom. She was trying her best to be composed, but it wasn't easy. What on earth did one do in a situation like this? She was sorry for Byron and she felt like such a criminal, but she had had no way of knowing it was him bending over her. She had acted in self-defense. She had to protect herself, didn't she? But what did she do now?

If he were badly hurt . . . but she couldn't let herself dwell on that. She would watch him for a while, and if he didn't come out of it or if his breathing became labored, she would make her way down to Karly's house and see if her phone worked. However, she was reasonably sure that the power was out everywhere in the area.

China gently bathed Byron's face and wound again with the wet cloth before she picked up one of the lamps and worked her way back to the bathroom to redampen the cloth. Then she returned and placed it on the injury.

When Byron began to shiver, she piled more wood on the fire, then started out of the room to get more blankets. She glanced back over her shoulder when she heard him groan. He was trying to get off the couch.

She rushed back to him and barely reached him in time to keep him from falling off. Sitting down on the edge of the couch, she held him to her, trying to warm him with her body heat.

When he wrapped his arms around her and began to mumble incoherently, China decided that in his arms wasn't the best place to be. She dragged a chair over in front of the couch. She was afraid to leave Byron long enough just to go down the hall for a blanket; the fire and the coverlet would have to do. For a few minutes she sat there before him, worried, frightened, concerned that he never would arouse fully.

His blond features were outlined in the flickering lamplight, and once again China saw how very handsome he was. She had never seen a man created quite so enticingly as this one, even though he was blond. No matter how she tried to wipe away the image of him as he had looked when she had undressed him, she could not. She recalled vividly how handsome he had been with the firelight flickering over the muscular contours of his body and glistening in the golden highlights of his hair. Abruptly she recalled seeing Byron on this couch with Marlene, and for the first time China wondered what had become of the redhead.

Suddenly she recalled that she was supposed to be keeping Byron awake, and she began to question him again. "Where's Marlene?" she made herself ask.

Byron didn't seem to know. "Marlene," he muttered. "My head." He reached up again to touch it. "My head hurts."

"I know. I know," China said soothingly, "but you're going to be all right. Really you are." She grimaced, then looked up at the heavens. "Please, let him be all right."

"Where have you been, Byron?" she asked to keep him awake.

"I've been—hell, I don't know. My head hurts."

China reached out and stroked his face gently, and he smiled a little.

"That feels better." Then he tried to focus on her. "Sara?"

"Who the hell is Sara?" she muttered irritably to herself. "No wonder he didn't consider Marlene his mistress. No telling how many of his women there are."

"Marlene?" he murmured, having finally registered the name.

"No—Daisy," she retorted irritably.

"Daisy?"

"Damn," she muttered. "I've hit on another one. I should have said Buttercup. But he probably knows that one too."

Then, feeling remorse because she knew he was confused enough without her adding to it, she said softly, "It's China. You're back in the cabin, Byron. You've suffered a nasty blow to your head, but you'll be fine."

"I hurt my head," he murmured in a slurred voice.

"Yes," she agreed, "but your headache will soon be gone."

"Get me something for this headache, will you, Sara?"

China tightened her lips in displeasure, but she knew she was being foolish to feel annoyance at being called another woman's name. "Not now. Just lie there."

She recalled that the doctor hadn't wanted Randolph to take any medication. Time dragged almost unbearably as China tried to think of things to say to Byron to keep him awake. Much to her chagrin, he called her several other women's names, and he kept trying to sleep; but, tired though she was herself, she kept talking to him until she was hoarse. When she ran out of questions to ask him, she began to tell him stories about her own life.

Time wore on until finally almost three hours had passed. It seemed like an eternity to China as she sat there in that stiff chair, not daring to take her eyes off the man before her. Finally he drifted into sleep and she let him. She was reasonably sure she had kept him awake long enough. He shifted once, moving from his back to his side again, and she reached out to cover him up, acutely aware that he was naked beneath the cover.

One of his long legs was protruding from the coverlet, but there wasn't enough blanket to go around, and China gave up trying to keep all of him wrapped up. She heard the old mantel clock strike one. She went back to the fire and put more wood on it, grateful that someone had had the foresight to bring in piles of it and stack them on the hearth.

After she had returned to her chair, she stared at Byron again. The sight of him lying there, helpless, nude, and hurt, really did make her heart beat faster. She wished the night would pass quickly. She could better decide what to do in the daylight, when she could see how bad the storm damage was. She would have to drive to the nearest neighbor, or perhaps all the way into town, and get some help.

She was exhausted herself, and although she dozed from time to time, she didn't dare go to bed, leaving him alone. She must have nodded off for a few minutes because at about five o'clock something awakened her. As she gazed worriedly at Byron he rolled onto his back, and the motion caused him to groan deeply. Her pulse beating wildly at her temples, China watched as his gray eyes slowly opened. "Oh, thank God," she said aloud, exhaling a deep breath.

Dazed eyes gradually focused on her as she leaned forward. Byron stared at her for a moment, then raised his hand to his head.

"Don't touch it," China cautioned.

"What happened?" Byron muttered. "I feel like I've been hit with a sledgehammer."

China glanced away. "I thought you were a burglar. I hit you with the pitcher of flowers that was on the coffee table."

Byron stared at her. "You did *what?*" He shook his head, then reached up to touch it. "I don't remember a thing, but I've got a devil of a headache."

Before China could explain again and apologize, Byron spotted his clothes scattered around the floor. He raised the coverlet to peer down at his nude body.

"China, you naughty girl," he drawled. "You've stripped me —and heaven knows what else. You didn't have to knock me out to do this. We could have talked about it. I'm sure we could have worked something out so that we both could have enjoyed it."

"I see that you've recovered," China said dryly, but she could feel the color rising to her face. She remembered all too clearly every line of his body as it had looked when she hastily undressed him.

"Boy, do you pack a wallop," he said thickly. "My head feels like it's coming off."

"I'm sorry," she murmured contritely. "I didn't know it was you. You should have called out to me."

"Before or after you hit me?" he asked with a hint of a grin.

74

"Before, if you had any sense."

"I didn't know you were in here."

"I didn't know *you* were in here either," she replied. She did feel guilty, but not nearly as guilty as she had before she saw that he was all right.

"I've heard of candlelight courting," he said lightly, "but if you've finished with me, can we have some lamplight in here?"

"The power is out," she replied tartly. "Otherwise, I assure you, we wouldn't be here like this."

"No?" His gray eyes were teasing in the shadowy light. "Where would we be? If you have something more in mind, let me know. I'd like to participate this time."

"You did participate in everything that went on," she said firmly.

"Everything, China?" he asked suggestively.

"Yes, everything! You got your head bashed in, didn't you?"

He touched the bump. "Don't remind me. It really aches."

Feeling remorseful again, China stood up. "I'll try to find something to ease the pain. I believe there's aspirin in the medicine cabinet; it should be all right to give it to you now."

When she rose, Byron saw for the first time how beautifully she was gowned. The red satin caught the firelight, and China was gorgeously outlined for him to see. The gown was cut daringly low—the *V* went all the way to her waist—and he drew in his breath as he saw the gentle swell of her high, firm breasts and the abundance of cleavage displayed. Her pointed nipples jutted against the sleek material covering them. As she moved past the couch, Byron reached out and caught her arm.

"Maybe you could kiss me and make the hurt go away."

Gazing back down at him, China let her dark eyes whip over him. "No, I don't think so," she said. "You lie still and rest. Try to cool your ardor for once."

"Why, China, you surprise me. I'm just a normal man with normal desires. Surely you must know that by now. When I see a woman dressed like you are"—his gray eyes roved over her assessingly, taking in the sexy gown—"I simply can't help but respond normally."

"Try just a little harder," she retorted sarcastically.

"Oh, believe me, I am trying, but I just can't help myself.

75

Don't leave me," he said, pulling her down in front of him on the couch. "I'm afraid of the dark, and I need you."

He reached up and gently outlined the shape of her full lips with a single fingertip; then, before China could resist, he drew her down to him to kiss her mouth eagerly. His lips moved hungrily against hers, and his hands made enticing circles on her back, which was barely protected by the rich satin.

Her hair fell forward in a dark curtain, and Byron reached up to let his fingers run through it provocatively while his mouth continued its skilled seduction of China's.

"Byron," she finally managed to protest against his caressing lips, "you shouldn't be doing this. You don't feel well."

"I feel just fine now, and so do you," he murmured huskily.

His fingers found their way into the deep *V* of her gown and circled the peaks of her breasts, causing her nipples to respond instantly, enticing her into the eddy of his rising desire. His mouth spilled kisses down her pale throat, and although she tried to draw away from him, she was quickly succumbing to his provocative caresses. When Byron freed one swelling breast from the gown and his lips closed around the taut tip, waves of fire rushed through China's body, burning away any resistance she might have had to his touch. She could feel the hunger begin to grow inside her, and when she reached out to touch Byron's body, she remembered that he was naked beneath the coverlet.

Her hands spread out over the thick hair covering his muscular chest, and she gripped it tightly, relishing the crisp feel of it beneath her fingertips.

Byron moved to ease her down onto the couch with him, and suddenly he groaned deeply. His cry of pain brought China abruptly back to the present, and she pulled free of his embrace.

"I'm sorry," he said with a short laugh. "It doesn't seem to be my night for love. I'm afraid we're going to have to postpone it for a bit. My head hurts so damned bad."

China felt like striking him because he had so easily lured her into his arms and because he was so darned confident that she would succumb completely to him. But then, what else was he to think?

"You needn't bother yourself about it," she said casually, her

76

tone covering her pounding heart and quick breathing. "I have no intention of letting you take more than a kiss."

"Take?" he repeated. "You seemed willing enough. I thought we were both enjoying it."

"You thought wrong." She stood up. She knew she had to get away from him before he caused her to do something else foolish. She had too much pride to be one woman in a line of several. She had already had that experience, and she had learned her lesson well.

"What happened to Marlene?"

Byron laughed softly. "She wasn't too taken with you and our little cabin. She decided she had better things to do elsewhere. I'm afraid you've effectively strained my relationship with that lady."

"So you come back here to try to make it with me," China said coldly. "Is that it?"

He laughed again. "Yes, I suppose that was the idea." There was no point in making the same excuses to her that he had made to himself. He hadn't come back to talk about the house. He had come because she was here. Incredibly he hadn't been able to get her out of his mind. But once again she had thrown a wrench into his plans. He had heard of being bowled over by a woman, but he hadn't intended to be knocked out by one. He couldn't make love to her now if his life depended on it.

China could feel the anger rising inside her. She had told herself that he was that kind of man, but she was disappointed to have him confirm it. She had wanted something more from him—what, she wasn't quite sure, but she was angry that he had dismissed Marlene, then returned, expecting her to tumble into his arms.

"Who do you think you are, mister?" she said in an insulted but controlled voice. "Do you really think you can crawl out of one woman's arms and then into mine? Worse yet, do you think you can make love with one woman right here in my granny's house, then come back here and seduce me?"

Byron didn't like the sound of it when she put it like that. That wasn't what had happened; if only she knew. He had had no intention of making love to her—ever. He had heard of her for years, but he hadn't been interested. Was it his fault that he had seen her and gotten caught up in her spell? She attracted him terribly. She wasn't his type at all, but right now, with her standing there, so angry and so beautiful, he would give one of his restaurants if he could claim her.

"I plead innocent," he said in a joking tone. "I had no intention of making love to you at all. I've told you before that you're not my type, but—"

China didn't wait for him to finish his explanation. "Good," she said savagely. "At least we're in agreement on something." She moved away from him. "I'll go get some medication for your head." Then she rushed from the room.

As she hurried down the dark hall she realized that she had forgotten to take the lamp with her. She could see very little in the scant morning light, but she wouldn't go back for the lamp.

"Damn him to hell," she muttered. Had he just been playing with her when he kissed her? Well, one thing was certain: He was an arrogant son of a gun, and she'd be damned if she would let him touch her again. She didn't need his caresses. There were plenty of men who considered her "their type."

In the dark she hunted around until she found something that might be an aspirin bottle, then returned to the living room. Byron had dragged himself up on a pillow that he had propped on the couch arm.

"Here," China said, shoving the bottle at him.

Byron stared at it. "Could I impose on you for a drink of water? Those things are kind of hard to take dry." He could see that she didn't give a damn, and he was sorry he had made her angry again. He wanted to try to finish his explanation, but he knew it would be like flogging a dead horse at this point.

This time China remembered the lamp, and a few minutes later she returned with a glass of water.

"Thanks," Byron said gently.

"You're welcome." Her voice was strained, and he wanted nothing more than to take her in his arms again, but that was what had gotten him in trouble before. He would have to take his time with her. And there would be plenty of it. Neither of them was going anywhere in this weather with the roads as they were. The thought made him smile, and when he handed the glass back to her, his fingers lightly brushed hers.

78

"I'm going to bed," she said, turning away from him. She didn't know what was wrong with her. She was fresh from a broken engagement with Dereck. He was the man who occupied her thoughts. But being here with Byron—She wouldn't let herself indulge in crazy thoughts.

When she heard Byron move, she looked back to see him attempting to stand up. "What are you doing?" she cried, pushing him back down on the couch.

"Going to the bedroom," he said. "Mine—not yours."

China bit back a sharp retort. "I believe you'd be better off staying right where you are awhile longer. I don't think you should try to walk."

His gray gaze raked over her. "Will you stay with me?"

"Absolutely not. I need some sleep."

"I'll be cold," he said in a low, suggestive voice.

"You need to cool off," she countered. But she was afraid he really would get cold when the fire burned down low. "I'll get more cover for you." With that, she moved away, once again forgetting the lamp. It angered her that Byron was able to make her forget everything, but there was no helping it. She made her way to Granny's bedroom. At least a little of the light from the front room followed her down the hall, and she was able to discern the bed.

When she reached for the heavy quilt that covered it, Demon suddenly leaped down and darted toward the hall. China sucked in her breath in alarm, then let it out in a heavy sigh. She would be glad when this night was over. It was one of the longest she could ever remember. Quilt in hand, she returned to the front room to find Demon, his yellow eyes glowing strangely, on the couch with Byron.

She wanted just to drop the cover down on them, but she made herself spread it out over man and cat. Byron was watching her, smiling slightly, and she could feel the warmth of his gaze. When she pulled the cover up around his neck and shoulders, she had the oddest sensation that he was going to try to kiss her again. But he didn't.

"Good night," she murmured.

"Good night, China."

She tossed a few more logs on the fire, then took the lamp in hand. Making herself remember that he was injured, she said to him, "If you want me, call me."

"I do want you," he said in a low voice. "But you'll have to give me a rain check. I'm not up to anything strenuous right now."

His words sent a shiver over her skin, but China wouldn't let herself think about that. Without another word she went to the guest bedroom. For a long time that night she lay in her bed thinking about Byron Scott.

China awakened early to another gloomy day. She opened her eyes and gazed around the room. It was late, she knew, and although she hadn't slept nearly enough, she couldn't sleep any longer. She had dreamed strange dreams when she did sleep, dreams about Byron and the cat and Blue and Randolph Davis. Stretching tiredly, she willed herself to get up. She had to see— no, *wanted* to see—how Byron was this morning.

When she had pulled her red robe on, she silently opened her door and made her way to the living room as quietly as she could. Byron was still sleeping, his tall form cramped and bent on the old Victorian couch. The fire had died out completely. Demon had deserted his master and was curled up in the chair. China crept closer, suddenly concerned that Byron might have worsened in the ensuing hours. She was happy to see that the light was on; the power had been restored and she could see Byron's features clearly. He was so still and quiet.

Demon awakened and eyed her suspiciously, but he didn't run away this time. China went to lean down over Byron's sleeping form. He turned over on his back, then tensed, as though aware that someone was observing him.

China moved away, but Byron had sensed her presence. "Good morning," he said in a husky voice. "How are you?"

"I'm fine. The question is, how are you?"

He yawned wearily. "I don't know yet. I'm not fully awake, but I had a hell of a night. I slept, but every time I turned over, my head ached so badly that it awakened me."

"I *am* sorry," China stressed.

"How sorry?"

"Oh, really, Byron, what more do you expect me to say?"

80

"That you feel sorry for me, that you have a little compassion for a man you almost killed," he teased lightly.

Embarrassed, China lowered her dark eyes. Her long lashes fluttered gently. "I do feel sorry for you." She looked at him. "I'm going to build a fire for you, then I'll cook breakfast. Will that make up for the damage?"

"Can you cook?"

"As well as you, I imagine," she retorted without thinking.

"Bet you can't," he teased. "I own all those restaurants, remember? I'm famous for the dishes I cook. Tell you what: You build the fire back up and *I'll* go cook breakfast."

Before China could protest, Byron had swung his legs over the side of the couch. She was about to glance away, sure that he didn't remember he wasn't dressed, when suddenly he lay back down on the couch.

"This head," he complained. "I'm so dizzy."

China frowned. She was certain that he needed to see a doctor. The rain had stopped, but she didn't know what the situation was outside. She started toward the window.

"Where are you going?" Byron asked.

"To see how bad it is out. I really think you need a doctor."

"No, thanks. I'll be fine. It feels like I almost got a concussion. I had one once when I played college football. What I need is bed rest. Anyway," he reasoned, "no one can get in or out of here. The dirt road leading to the house is a river of mud. My car is stuck on it."

"Of all times," she muttered to herself. She knew that the road could and did wash out, but it complicated matters so terribly now. "Are you sure you're all right?" she questioned worriedly.

"As all right as I'm going to be for a while." He tried to smile, but the attempt failed. "I think I'll go to the bathroom and clean up a little. Then I'm going into the other bedroom. This couch is so damned short. One night was bad enough, but two were two too many."

Smiling a little, China bent down over him. She had thought he had slept here that first night, but she was glad to have him confirm it. "Don't tell me your problems," she said in a joking voice. "I can't help it if your woman kicked you out of bed."

"I told you, she's not my woman," he said. "But she was the only one who slept in the bedroom after you turned up. I also told you that you effectively cooled my ardor for that lady. We were, and still are, only friends."

China realized how much she wanted to believe him. "You and Marlene didn't look like friends when I walked in on you," she replied. "I've heard of kissing cousins, but if your relationship with Marlene is platonic, I'll eat my rain hat."

"Now, that I would like to see," Byron drawled, "but nevertheless, Marlene and I are just friends. We have been for years. I'll admit that things were beginning to heat up a bit when you interrupted us, but we both decided that our friendship was too important to tamper with."

China told herself that he wouldn't miss one woman; after all, there was Sara and who knew who else; but before she could reply, Byron struggled to stand up, and her attention was drawn back to the matter at hand.

"Here, let me help you," she offered.

"I can manage," he insisted.

"Maybe," she said, "and maybe not. I'm concerned that you'll fall, and I know I'd never be able to lift you."

"But you would try, wouldn't you?" he prodded lightly.

Ignoring his teasing, China put her arm around his shoulders. "Hang on to the coverlet. You don't have any clothes on, remember?"

"So what's to hide?" he murmured. "You've seen it all already."

"Byron, please," she said sharply. "Will you make an effort to behave yourself?"

"Every effort." Again he sat up, sliding his feet carefully to the floor, then wrapping the coverlet around him like a toga. His head was still swimming and he was dizzy, but not too dizzy to appreciate how lovely China looked in her red sleepwear in the brightness of daylight.

He let her help support him, his arm around her shoulder while she put both of hers around his waist, and slowly they made their way to the bathroom. The floor was cold, and Byron was eager to get back to bed.

When he had finished in the bathroom, China helped him to

the bedroom. He was walking more easily now, the dizziness not as bad as it had been when he had first attempted to get up. He was certain he would be perfectly safe without China's help, but he still wanted her by his side.

He eased down on the old feather mattress, then stretched out, and before China could escape, Byron pulled her down on top of him. "I thought about you half the night," he murmured against her lips.

China stared down into his gray eyes. "Let me up, Byron. You're injured, remember? Besides, you don't like my type—and I don't like yours."

For a moment Byron was taken aback by her declaration. He liked her type exceptionally well, he had discovered, and he intended to see that she liked his. Her warm, shapely curves were pressing against him, and he was all too aware that he had nothing on beneath the crocheted coverlet. He could feel his body responding to hers, and when he was better, he meant to see that he stirred her blood as much as she stirred his.

CHAPTER SIX

Smiling enigmatically, Byron murmured, "Will you play nurse for me today? You could examine me all over if you'd like."

"I wouldn't," China declared. "Now, let me up."

Abruptly, Byron freed her, but he was still smiling at her as she slid off his body and started out of the room.

China glanced back at him once, in time to see him take the coverlet off and slide under the blankets on the bed. She could feel her face flame afresh as she recalled the detailed lines of his muscular body, and she quickened her steps.

As she made her way toward the guest room to pick up Blue, she couldn't help but recall that she had already seen every part of Byron's body. She hadn't examined it, that was true, but she had a feeling that it would be a heady experience to do so.

Blue was delighted to be uncovered, and he began his morning serenade with extra exuberance. China took him on her finger and when she spoke to him in an animated voice, saying, "Hello there, fat feathers," he responded with "Hello there yourself, fat feathers."

"Well, I don't blame you," China said, uttering nonsense to him, for the bird was only parroting another phrase she had taught him. "I wouldn't like to be called fat either."

Suddenly she looked down at the floor and saw that Demon was slyly creeping toward the two of them, his ears laid back, his shoulders hunched forward.

"No!" she screamed. "No!" She tried to shove Blue back in his cage just as the cat leaped up toward the bird, and the frightened parrot lifted his wings in flight, soaring out of the room and down the hall. Demon went in swift pursuit.

As China fled down the hall after them, she heard Byron call out, "What's wrong?"

She had no time for his questions. Blue, panting as though he might die from fright at any moment, had landed on top of the curtains at the living-room window. Demon was already trying to scale them, his sharp claws effectively gripping the sheer fabric as he climbed upward.

Furious, China grasped him by the scruff of the neck as she had seen Byron do and dragged him from the curtains, shredding the sheer material in the process. Now Demon, too, was terrified; he hissed and swiped at the air dangerously.

"Here, I'll take him."

China spun around to see Byron, his lower body wrapped in the coverlet, standing unsteadily before her. His broad chest was matted with thick blond hair, and even his shoulders and arms were covered with it. The man was just too darn appealing.

"You shouldn't be out of bed," she said sharply, taking out her frustrations on him.

"I thought you might need help."

"I don't," she flung at him. "What I need is for you and this

84

beast to get out of this house. I've had nothing but trouble since I found you here."

As Byron stood watching the angry dark-haired woman he was reminded that he liked Colleen Castleberry's little grand-daughter—a lot. This tall woman with a hard shell that barely covered her sensitive nature, this woman with her sexually frustrated parrot, this woman who had cracked him over the head, then sat up most of the night caring for him—for some strange reason she really appealed to him.

He found it amusing that she wasn't interested in the fact that he was wealthy; if anything, his string of restaurants only annoyed her because it made her realize that he could afford any house he wanted. She couldn't know that he was attracted to the old cabin because she owned the other half of it. *Tenants in common,* he believed was the term. Well, he meant to see that they developed other things in common.

"Don't be too hard on us," Byron murmured. "Demon was just acting naturally. It's instinctive for him to go after birds. He's a predatory animal."

"And is that what you are too?" China demanded.

Holding on to the coverlet with one hand, Byron approached and took Demon from her. "Isn't that really what your problem is?" he asked softly. "You see me as a predatory animal and you don't know if you can handle me."

"I don't know what you're talking about," she snapped. But she did know. She felt as vulnerable with Byron as she knew Blue was with Demon. She was attracted to him, but she knew he had about as many scruples as his cat. Hadn't he come back here with the intention of seducing her? And hadn't she almost let him?

Byron's gray gaze held hers, and when China saw how pale he looked, she turned away. "Go back to bed," she ordered. "You shouldn't be up."

Hugging her arms to her body, she walked to the window and looked out. The rain was pouring down again. She didn't know when she would ever get to leave this house. She still felt that Byron should be checked by a doctor, but there was nothing to be done about that. She glanced back to speak to him but saw that he was already gone.

85

Sighing heavily, she stared out at the dark day and wondered when it would stop raining. How long would she be shut up here in this cabin with this man and this animal? And what could it lead to? A pang of guilt shot through her when she heard Blue begin to cluck softly.

She looked up at him. "Come on down, sweetie," she coaxed, holding out her hand so that he would have a perch. "It's all right. Come on down."

But the frightened parrot gazed back at her helplessly. He was too scared to come down. China sighed again. She would have to go up and get him. She glanced around the room, seeking something high enough to stand on. Finally she settled for a chair, but when she had dragged it over to the window, she found that no amount of enticing would get the bird to leave the safety of the curtain rod. Instead he ran toward the other end.

"Oh, damn," she muttered, gazing at him impotently. "What are we doing here with that blond man and that black beast? You and I were supposed to spend a quiet time here, and look at this mess. You're upset; I'm upset. Now what am I going to do?"

Climbing down, China walked over to the couch and took the two pillows off it so she would be eye level with the parrot. After she had stacked them on the chair, she again tried to reach Blue. When that didn't work, she kicked off her shoes and perched precariously on the slender wooden arms of the chair.

She held out her hand and coaxed him forward in her gentlest voice, and finally the reluctant parrot stepped out onto her index finger. China moved to get down off one of the chair arms, but when she did she lost her balance, and the chair toppled over sideways with her and Blue still on it.

Her first priority was Blue, and she tossed him off her finger just as she hit the floor with a thud. The parrot gave a cry of alarm and began to run toward the couch as fast as his little feet would carry him. He had had too much drama for one morning, and he simply wanted to hide. China watched as he fled under the couch, but she was helpless to do anything for herself, much less the bird. She had landed on her back, and the fall had knocked the breath out of her.

She was still trying to catch her breath when Byron appeared again in the flowered coverlet. He rushed toward her, bending down and easily lifting her in his arms. She wanted to protest, but she was still gasping for breath.

"China," he exclaimed. "What happened?"

She wanted to tell him to put her down—and she would have if she could catch her breath and speak. But before that happened, Byron had carried her over to the couch and set her down on it.

He stood there beside her, looking absurd in the coverlet that was wrapped around his middle, one end tucked in as if he were in a big bath towel, leaving his upper body naked. He frowned worriedly as he began to check her over. He was examining her for broken bones when she was finally able to breathe normally.

Suddenly she burst into laughter. As Byron looked at her strangely she shook her head. "Oh, Byron, we're a fine pair, you and I. This is turning into a comedy of errors. First you, then me."

She struggled to sit up, exposing a long length of shapely leg in the process, and Byron pressed her back down against the cushions with firm fingers. "I'm fine. Really, I am. You're the one who should be lying down. I just got the breath knocked out of me. I fell off the chair."

Her rich red peignoir had parted, and Byron reached out to stroke the curve of her leg. "Are you sure you didn't hurt yourself?" he asked thickly. He was suddenly remembering how enticing she had been the previous night as he held her in his arms, and how much he had wanted her.

China watched as his hand traveled up the silky skin of her thigh, and she shivered involuntarily at his warm touch. She had wanted Byron last night so badly that she had burned with hunger for him. She couldn't let that happen again. She wasn't ready for it, but abruptly Byron sat down on the couch beside her and leaned down to claim her mouth in fiery possession.

His full lips moved against hers persuasively, coaxingly, as he drew her against his chest, his hands moving gently over her back. China tried her best to hang on to sanity, but she was being lured into the depths of desire by Byron's tantalizing caresses. She could feel her heart pounding, and in a last attempt

87

to save herself from surrender to his charms, she pushed at his shoulders.

Her defensive move only served to make her more aware of him, for her palms burned where they touched his naked skin, and her fingers spread out hungrily over the muscular contours. She ached to draw him to her rather than drive him away. She was acutely aware that he was nude beneath the coverlet and that it covered only the bare essentials.

She was breathless as he pulled back to study her with his smoldering gray gaze. Staring at him, momentarily caught between her desire to escape and her desire to have him claim her, she had a difficult time remembering that she was the one who had interrupted the loving. Her parted lips trembled rebelliously as she tried to form some protest against his seduction.

Byron reached out and traced her mouth with his index finger, and China could feel her erratic breathing at this new and subtle assault on her senses. When he slid his finger in between her lips, she involuntarily opened her mouth wider. He traced the edges of her teeth, then lightly stroked her moist tongue.

The movement was so erotic that China's lips closed down possessively, sucking lightly. Byron slid his finger out of her mouth and began to trail it down the slender column of her throat while China watched, hypnotized by his magnetism. He traced the V of her robe, his sensitive touch sending shivers over her skin as he barely caressed her partially exposed breast. He strayed from his route to trace the fullness, circling it tantalizingly, the circles growing smaller and smaller until they had ringed China's throbbing nipple.

Her head lowered, her eyes downcast, China watched the sensuous movement, her pounding heart and breathlessness making her breasts rise and fall provocatively. With each passing moment Byron was stirring her senses so deeply that she could hardly believe he was only barely touching her.

He continued to follow the deep V, again straying long enough to set China on fire as he gently circled her other breast. She could feel every nerve in her body responding as Byron teased her nipple, then left it.

When Byron had completed outlining the V, he tilted China's head back with his finger. He looked into her eyes briefly before his mouth closed on hers. She forgot that she had meant to turn away from him. She forgot that she had promised herself not to succumb to his seduction.

She was burning all over. She didn't want any more teasing touches. She wanted him to hold her, to kiss her, to make love to her, to ease the hungry ache washing through her in waves.

His hands slid down possessively over her breasts, sending a fresh fever racing in China's blood. When he untied the ribbon holding her robe together, exposing her gown, she shivered under his exploring fingers.

From somewhere she was vaguely aware of Blue calling out to her softly, his cry still distressed, but her brain was too foggy from Byron's caresses to function properly. When the frightened clucking occurred again, this time louder and more pathetic, China abruptly remembered that she had come in here to rescue the panicked bird. He had run under the couch when she had fallen off the chair, and the poor little thing was still there in his anguish. And she was in Byron Scott's arms, on the verge of surrendering totally to his potent seduction.

"Oh, no!" she cried, struggling free of his embrace to scramble off the cushions. She didn't know who needed rescuing most, herself or Blue. Before Byron could draw her back to him, she was on her hands and knees, peering under the couch.

Byron stared down at her for a moment, relishing the view. China's breasts were partially exposed, and her shapely derriere was provocatively outlined in the red satin nightwear. Byron told himself that she was perhaps the loveliest woman he had ever seen. He could almost imagine how it would feel to kiss her breasts, to have those long, lovely legs wrapped around his waist, to lose himself in her warmth and beauty.

"Blue," she was calling softly. "Oh, Blue, come here."

"Demon is shut up in the library," Byron said. "You don't have to worry about him."

China looked up, a little relieved by that information, but she still had to get the parrot out and calm him down. "Come on, sweetie," she coaxed.

"Won't I do?" Byron murmured as he knelt down on the floor by her.

"No," she said emphatically. When she saw where his gaze

was resting, she straightened up a little and attempted to draw her robe about her. But the outfit wasn't designed for modesty, and her efforts proved futile. She leaned back on her heels. "Will you please go back to bed. You really shouldn't be up. And look at you—half dressed . . ." Her tone was accusing, even though she knew he had nothing else to wear.

She glanced around the room. His clothing was still scattered about where she had flung it when she had undressed him the night before. Even his navy shorts were carelessly tossed on top of his pants.

Byron went over and began to gather up his clothes. They were a mess, wrinkled and muddy.

"I'll do that if you'll just go back to bed," China said.

Unexpectedly, Blue walked out from under the couch and started climbing up the front of China's nightgown, holding on with his beak and his claws. "Hello, pretty baby," she said.

"Lucky bird," Byron murmured, but then he let his clothes fall from his hands, stood up, and left the room.

China was still shaking her head as she went back to her room and put Blue in his cage. Then she took the cage to the kitchen and began to cook breakfast.

The familiarity of the routine soon made the bird behave normally, and he began to make his usual chatter, repeating his favorite phrase, "Thanks a lot," until China responded with "Thanks a lot, yourself."

She was relieved to see that he was all right, and amazingly she found herself feeling sorry for the black cat shut up all alone in the library. But there was no help for it. She didn't want a repeat of what had just happened.

While the bacon and eggs were cooking, she put some seed and clean water in Blue's cage, then found a tray to put Byron's plate on. He had had a hectic morning himself, and she knew that he should be resting. He seemed to be fine, but she was still concerned. After all, she had been the one to hurt him and she did feel responsible.

When she had put food for both of them on plates and poured cups of steaming hot coffee, she put some bacon and eggs in a small dish and took them to the errant cat. Demon looked at her warily, but he was happy to get the food. China left a dish of water for him. Then she returned to the kitchen.

She wasn't really surprised to see that Byron was sleeping by the time she went back into Granny's room with the food. He had had quite a time of it recently. She smiled a little to herself. Byron Scott had certainly gotten more than he had bargained for when he tried to share her house with her.

She almost hated to wake him, but she knew he had to eat. When she had set the tray down on the table by the bed, she lightly shook his shoulder. "Byron."

Opening dazed gray eyes, he looked at her in bemusement. Then he sat up against the bed pillows, running his hands through his hair. "I must be more exhausted than I thought," he said. "I fell asleep."

"I know. Here. I have some breakfast for you."

"Mmm, it looks good. I'm starving. What time is it?"

China didn't really know. "It must be around eleven," she offered. She set the tray on the bed beside Byron and watched as he began to eat. He had long, attractive fingers and beautifully shaped hands, she noticed, and the memory of the touch of those hands in her hair and on her flesh caused her pulse to race.

"Damn," China muttered aloud. What was it about this man? Why was she always thinking of him in a physical way? He was the least likely man in the world to attract her. What was her interest in a wealthy blond playboy with a demon black cat?

"Nothing," she mumbled firmly. "Nothing at all."

"What's the matter?"

She glanced at him in surprise. She must have been speaking aloud again. She really was going to have to break herself of that habit of muttering. "Nothing."

China didn't see Byron smile as she returned to the kitchen for her own breakfast. When she went back to the bedroom, she sat down in a chair near the bed and, holding her tray on her lap, began to eat. Byron wasn't the only one who had had an incredible night, and she found she, too, was famished. It was late, and the last several hours had been full of excitement—excitement of all kinds, she reminded herself.

"I wonder if I could impose on you to feed Demon," Byron said. "He has cat food in the cupboard."

"I gave him the same thing we're having. I hope you don't mind."

Byron shook his head. "No, of course not. Thank you. You may think he's a rotten devil, but I rather like the ol' boy."

"You would," she retorted. But she understood. Byron was right about the cat: Demon had acted instinctively. If she didn't have Blue along with her, she was sure there would be no problem at all. Except that the real problem was Byron.

A rush of shame flooded her face with bright color as she remembered her original purpose in coming here. She should have already become Mrs. Dereck Morehouse. She should be somewhere in Europe, waking up next to Dereck. Instead she was here in Granny's old cabin, thinking about this stranger—and *only* about him, she reminded herself. If she had loved Dereck so deeply, how could she forget him the minute she was face-to-face with another man?

"Penny for your thoughts," Byron murmured.

China glanced down at her bacon, took a bite, and procrastinated as she ate it. "I was thinking about my fiancé," she said firmly. After all, that was true. She had just realized that she *should* have been thinking about Dereck.

"I see." Byron picked up his toast and bit into it. So China's ex-fiancé was still on her mind. Damn, he had forgotten all about that man. He himself was already foolishly making plans for China. But he didn't want the ghost of some past lover hovering around them. Still, he knew she wasn't the kind of woman to forget in a matter of days a man she had intended to marry.

Byron didn't mean to become seriously involved with her himself; he had already told her that he wasn't the marrying kind. He liked her. He wanted her. He thought they would be good together, could enjoy some time with each other. But he couldn't think of anything more unpleasant than having her accept his attentions on the rebound from her lost love. He didn't want to be used as a catharsis for her unhappiness over another man.

He frowned. This was going to be more complicated than he

had anticipated. He found that he desired her greatly. And he wanted her to desire him, to *like* him. He knew he hadn't made a very good impression so far. But he would rectify that.

"So, tell me about your elusive man," Byron said. He didn't want to hear about her lover, but he knew the information would be important to him if he hoped to win her affection.

Shrugging with pretended carelessness, she replied lightly, "There's nothing to tell. It didn't work, that's all."

Byron read all the signs of her distress, and it bothered him. She had stopped eating and her ivory skin was paler. She wouldn't look him in the eyes.

"What didn't work?" he persisted, feeling like a heel for prying so relentlessly yet unable to stop himself. He really wanted to know about her relationship with her ex-fiancé and whether or not she seriously intended to put the man in her past. He also wondered if it was possible.

This time China met his eyes levelly. "It's really none of your business."

Byron made himself grin. "That's true, China, but we've already bared ourselves to each other—physically, I mean—and I thought it might be nice to get to know each other in different ways."

China had to smile, even though she was embarrassed to remember that, not only had she undressed him last night, but he had also seen her naked in the bathtub. And it was true that they knew very little about each other. She knew only that he was disturbingly attractive, had too many women in his life, owned half her house and a number of restaurants, and had a black cat as tenacious as he was.

"I was engaged to Dereck for two years. Twice we set the wedding date." She paused thoughtfully. "Or maybe *I* was the only one who did that," she amended. "The first time Dereck called off the ceremony, pleading that he wasn't quite ready for marriage." She glanced away, then met his eyes again, feeling ashamed. "The second time I called off the wedding, realizing that Dereck still wasn't ready—that he never would be ready."

For a moment Byron gazed at her thoughtfully. "Do you love him?" he asked.

China laughed bitterly. "No, I suffered through two major disappointments in my life because I hate him."

Byron grinned sheepishly. It had been a stupid question. He supposed he had wanted her to say that she didn't love Dereck anymore. Obviously that wasn't the case: She had instantly gone behind her protective shell and responded sarcastically because she still loved the man.

He knew he was a fool to become involved with her, but as he looked at her he told himself that he wanted to be the one to make her forget Dereck. He wanted to be the one to make her love again, to make it good for her, as he knew he could.

But there was only one thing wrong: He didn't want marriage any more than Dereck apparently did, and he had a feeling that the cottage by the side of the road and the flowers and children were an integral part of this woman's dream of love.

He laughed lightly. Maybe he was being arrogant again. China had responded to his kisses, but other than that, she hadn't shown any sign that she found him attractive, much less so irresistible that she might want to marry him. To say that his thoughts were premature was an understatement. Why worry over something that was, in all probability, as remote as the moon?

"What's so funny?" China asked defensively.

Byron shook his head, suddenly serious. He certainly didn't find her revelation amusing. In fact, he thought Dereck sounded like a fool. If he ever made a commitment to this woman . . . He shook his head. What on earth was he thinking?

"Now it's your turn," China said unexpectedly. "Tell me about Sara and Daisy."

Byron was put on the defensive by the surprise question. "What about Sara?" He didn't know anyone named Daisy, but Sara was real enough and he wondered where China had gotten the name.

"You talked about her last night when you were laid out on the couch."

"You had no right to pump me about my life then," Byron said with a vehemence that startled China. She had struck a

94

nerve, and she saw that this man didn't take his women as lightly as she had suspected.

"I didn't pump you," she said evenly. "What little I knew about victims in the state you were in last night led me to believe that I shouldn't let you sleep for several hours. I tried to keep you awake; you were the one who brought up Sara."

"What did I say?" he demanded, his gray eyes blazing with sudden life.

China shrugged again. She wanted to keep him in suspense, but he was clearly upset by her mention of the woman, and now she was too curious to tease him or upset him further. "Nothing. You called me by her name several times."

Byron visibly relaxed, but his mind went spinning on a backward journey. So he still thought about Sara, even after all these years. Sara, with her long legs and dark brown hair. He had married—and divorced—her so long ago.

He smiled bitterly to himself. Was it fair to put it all so simply? Sara had decided he wasn't moving up in the world fast enough to please her. Money had been her god; Daddy had had plenty of it, but Byron wasn't earning it fast enough for her.

Sara had erroneously thought Byron had received a considerable portion of his family's fortune when he turned twenty-one. Only things hadn't worked like that in his family. His father had helped invest in his son's first restaurant, but after that he had been on his own.

And while he struggled to succeed, as much to please his beautiful jet-set wife as himself, Sara had been on her own too. It had been so many years ago, but just the memory of how he had felt when he found out she was sleeping with that Greek shipping tycoon caused his blood pressure to rise. He had really loved her; he had been so young and idealistic—just twenty-two then.

His gaze was drawn back to China. She was young and idealistic, too, and he promised himself that if they began an affair, he would level with her from the start.

He smiled suddenly, thinking of the ridiculousness of his thoughts. "What's so amusing?" she asked, staring at him suspiciously.

He shrugged. "Nothing. I was just thinking of how I'm going to make you fall in love with me."

"That *is* funny," she said without a trace of amusement in her voice. Then she stood up, her tray in one hand. "I'm finished with my breakfast. How about you? Shall I take your tray away?"

"Yes, thank you."

His fingers caught hers as she reached for the tray. Before China could drag her hand away, Byron had placed a kiss in her palm. Anxiously she looked into his gray eyes, and she saw the promise of more kisses to come. Desire was smoldering there, and before China could be burned by it, she quickly pulled her hand away. Then she picked up Byron's breakfast tray.

A tray in each hand, she walked regally from the room, but once she was outside his door, she leaned against the hallway wall, feeling a little dizzy from the kiss. Had Byron meant it when he said he would make her fall in love with him? Surely he was only teasing her. The only problem was that she *didn't* think it was funny. She had the feeling that it wouldn't take much to fall for him—not much at all—and the thought was more alarming than she cared to admit.

CHAPTER SEVEN

While China washed the breakfast dishes, Blue sat on her shoulder, offering comments and cries. "Hello there yourself, fat feathers," he called out.

"Who are you calling fat feathers?" China asked, picking up another cup and washing it. Suddenly she was struck by how domestic the whole scene seemed. Here she was, doing the dishes after she had had breakfast with Byron Scott here in their house.

"It's ridiculous. It's absurd. It's too crazy," she muttered to herself. "I shouldn't be here. He shouldn't be here. One of us shouldn't be here."

"Hello, pretty baby," Blue squawked, but China, lost in her own thoughts, kept muttering to herself.

She wasn't aware that Byron had gone down the hall to the bathroom and paused by the kitchen when he heard her voice. He pushed against the swinging door and looked in to find China and Blue carrying on two different conversations, both oblivious to the fact that one wasn't responding to the other.

For several minutes Byron stood there, watching the two of them, smiling to himself. He honestly couldn't decide what it was about China that he found so irresistible. But there was something; there was no doubt about that. Unexpectedly the fact troubled him, and he didn't know why it should. He was used to finding women attractive and making the most of it. Abruptly he let the door close and continued to the bathroom.

When China had finished the dishes, she went to the living room and gathered up Byron's clothes so that she could wash them. It was cold out in the laundry room, and she hastily put the garments into the washer on a gentle cycle, grateful that her father had talked Granny into getting some modern conveniences.

While the clothes were washing, she took Blue into the living room and cleaned a little in there, but she found her thoughts returning again and again to the cat. She was feeling sorrier and sorrier for poor Demon, who was still shut up in the library. Finally, to her annoyance, her conscience forced her to lock up the parrot and see about the other animal.

When she went to check on him, he was curled up in a chair, looking perfectly content, but she picked him up and took him to Byron's room so that he would have some company.

She smiled gently to herself after she had knocked on Byron's door and opened it. He was fast asleep again, looking like a little boy half buried under the covers. China set Demon down on the bed and left, closing the door behind her.

After she had returned to the living room, she tried the radio again and was happy to find some sentimental music from the forties. She loved the romantic old tunes, and she set about cleaning up the mud and mess Byron had made when he came in last night.

Then she got a broom and dustpan and cleaned up the debris from the broken pitcher. She couldn't recall a time when the old gray pitcher hadn't been there on the coffee table, filled with some kind of wild flowers. Granny would be disappointed to know that it had been destroyed.

"Ah, well, Granny," China murmured aloud. "It was all for a good cause." She smiled to herself. If one could call wounding an intruder who turned out to be Byron a good cause.

China glanced out the window and saw that the rain had finally stopped. Seeing the trees still dripping with water reminded her of Karly and Randolph in the little cabin hidden in the forest, and she went over to phone the old couple. In her concern over Byron she had forgotten all about them.

When Karly had assured her that Randolph was doing all right, China told the woman that she would be over a little later to visit. Karly seemed delighted and China hung up, then finished her chores. She put Byron's clothes in the dryer and returned to her room to find something to wear herself.

She selected a lovely fuchsia-colored dress with a row of tiny pearl buttons down the front. It wasn't really appropriate for the cabin, but she told herself that she had bought all these clothes and she was going to wear them. She knew the dress was especially flattering to her figure and coloring, but she wouldn't let herself think about that. She told herself firmly that she was putting it on for herself, not for Byron Scott.

By the time she had bathed and dressed for the day, complementing the dress with pale lavender shoes and a thick purple sweater that had been chosen as accessories, Byron's clothes were dry. China carefully folded them and took them to Granny's room. She didn't knock on the door this time; she just quietly stepped inside and laid everything but Byron's jacket on the chair by the bed. The jacket she hung on the back of the chair. Then she crept out and went the back way to Karly's house.

When Karly opened the door, she was smiling with pleasure, delighted to see her guest. China sniffed the air, smelling the wonderful aroma of sweets baking.

"What are you cooking? It smells heavenly."

"I'm fixing some cinnamon rolls for you and Randolph. Come on back to the kitchen."

China followed the old woman into the bright kitchen, which was done all in yellow, from the curtains to the floor. She had always loved this room when she visited. It had a huge old-fashioned hearth in which Karly had once cooked soups and other foods she could prepare in the big hanging pot that had now been banished to the front room to house a fern. A fire was burning, and China smiled at the picture of contentment Randolph made as he sat in front of the fireplace in a rocking chair, smoking his pipe.

"How are you?" she asked warmly.

A smile crinkled his mouth and lined the skin around his eyes. "I'm about as fit as an old fiddle. I was feeling a little rough, but I'm back on the road to recovery." He let his gaze roam over her. "And you are as pretty as ever. Come on over here. Don't you look lovely in that outfit?"

When China bent down to greet him, he hugged her warmly. "It's so good to have you back, honey. It gets a little lonely around here sometimes. You know, you're the closest thing to a child we have."

His sentimental words brought tears to her eyes. "It's good to be here," she told him, returning his hug.

"Well, let the child go before you squeeze the breath right out of her," Karly instructed, leaning down over the kitchen table to put the rich icing on the rolls. "Why don't you pour the coffee, China?" she said. "I'll get us a plate for these rolls."

Feeling right at home, China filled three cups with coffee and took them to the table. She was happy to be here with her old friends, and she was relieved to see that Randolph was feeling all right.

He joined them at the table, and as they ate, the talk inevitably turned to the storm and the power outage. "I was real worried about you being over there by yourself," Randolph told

China, "but Karly told me to stop my fussing. She said you could take care of yourself."

China smiled. "Truthfully the storm did make me a little nervous, but I'm not there by myself."

They both looked at her curiously. "What do you mean?" Karly asked.

China shook her head. "Byron. He came back."

"Well, I declare. You don't say." Her green eyes glowed a little. "That must mean you two are hitting it off."

China laughed. "Oh, we hit it off all right. He came back last night and I thought he was an intruder, so I hit him over the head with that gray pitcher of flowers."

"Oh, no!" Karly cried. "Did you hurt him bad? That old thing is heavy."

China smiled again. "The pitcher broke on his hard head. He's all right, but he had me worried for a while. I stunned him, I can tell you. He's sleeping now, but I really think he's fine."

"That's one way to get a man," Randolph said. "Knock him out."

"Randolph!" Karly admonished, glancing anxiously at China.

Randolph held up both hands. "Now, I didn't mean that like it sounded. You know I didn't."

China laughed, effectively easing the uncomfortable moment. "Well, I had to pay for my miscalculation. I really had my hands full. He was soaking wet and I had to undress him and put him to bed."

She had blurted it out before she thought about it, and when she saw Karly and Randolph exchange glances, she laughed again. Soon all three of them were laughing happily, talking about the incident, which definitely had its amusing side. But China did not mention the moment when Byron had drawn her into his arms.

Instead she talked about Demon and Blue, and the two old people conceded that that was an impossible situation. There was no way bird and beast could exist together, although Randolph said he'd heard of many cases in which they had been raised together from the beginning and got along just fine.

100

"I promise you, that isn't the case with Blue and Demon," China said.

The time passed so quickly that China was surprised when Karly said she had to start cooking supper. "You will stay and eat with us, won't you?"

"Oh, no, thank you. I'd better be getting back to Byron. What time is it, anyway?" She never seemed to know since she had arrived here in this remote and timeless area.

"Why, it's almost dark—after five."

"Poor Byron may be wondering what's happened to me," China said, "and I know Blue will be. I've got to get back over there." She was thoughtful for a moment. Suddenly she didn't want to find herself with the whole evening ahead of her alone with Byron. And she knew he couldn't leave; his car was still stuck in the mud. The road wouldn't dry out for a day or two.

"Karly, why don't you and Randolph come over to the house instead of cooking? I'll prepare something. It won't be much, but it'll do you both good to get out of the cabin for a while, and you can visit with Byron."

"I'd like that fine," Randolph said. "How about you, Karly?"

She nodded. "We'd appreciate that." She glanced down at the remaining cinnamon rolls. "I'll bring the dessert. Junior always liked these."

China nodded. "Great. See you in a little while." As she left the house she thought about Karly calling Byron "Junior." It was almost the most ridiculous name she could think of for a man who looked like him.

To her surprise, when she opened the back door to the house, she found that the aroma of cooking meat filled the room. Maybe she wouldn't have to cook dinner at all; Byron must be in the kitchen. She hurried a little, interested to see what he was up to.

The sight of him standing at the kitchen counter took her breath away. He had bathed, shaved, and dressed in the clean clothes, and he smelled of soap. He turned and grinned broadly at her when he heard her behind him.

"Hello. I woke up and wondered what had happened to you. I decided you must have gone to Karly's house." He motioned around the room with his hand. "I have dinner almost ready. I was about to go hunting for you."

China smiled to herself. There was no way to miss Byron's intention. He was planning an intimate dinner for two tonight, no doubt with food he was going to serve Marlene while they were at the cabin.

The round pine table was covered with a lace tablecloth, and two candles had been placed in the middle of it. A bottle of wine was chilling in an ice bucket, with two long-stemmed wine glasses standing nearby. China sniffed appreciatively. Byron had cooked some kind of beef dish that looked delicious, and he had steamed vegetables and baked hot biscuits to accompany it.

Amused, China said innocently, "How wonderful, Byron. I've invited Karly and Randolph to dinner. *I* was planning to cook, but this is better yet—all done for me."

Clearly, Byron was not pleased, and China was amazed that he covered for himself so well. "Boy, is that a relief," he said, pretending to wipe his brow. "I thought I was going to have to spend an intimate night here with you by myself." But immediately he walked over to the cupboard and took out another bottle of wine to put in the refrigerator. Then he got out two more glasses. China was sure Byron was cooling the second bottle for later in the evening, when the two of them would be alone again. Obviously, here was a man who could adapt to the moment and still plan for the future.

"I'll call them and tell them to come on over," China said. "This is all too lovely to let it spoil by allowing it to get cold."

"Yes," Byron muttered under his breath. "Things cool off here in a hurry."

"What did you say?" China asked.

"I said yes, do go and call them," Byron said, none too enthusiastically. China went into the living room, smiling to herself. The man really could be irresistible. Such a romantic setting he had planned—and wine, yet!

Karly and Randolph were even more delighted to learn that Byron had already done the cooking. Apparently he was no idle boaster, for they told her they had sampled his meals before, and they were eager to do so again.

China returned to the kitchen, where she found Byron setting

102

two more places at the table. She smiled a little to herself. At least he was good-natured; she liked that in a man. It appeared that he was also flexible, something she hadn't realized before, since he had been so obstinate about not selling her his half of the house.

"It all looks wonderful," she said. "You'd make a fine house-wife."

"Why, thank you, kind sir," he mocked, bowing low. "My only wish is to please you."

That she was beginning to believe, and it made her nervous. What was his real motive? Did he want to seduce her? To add her to his list of women? Or was he now determined to prove to her that *he* was *her* type? Clearly he wasn't used to being denied by the women on whom he chose to bestow his attentions.

In moments Karly and Randolph appeared at the back door, distracting China from her thoughts. They were beaming when she opened the door for them.

"This is so nice of you two," Karly said excitedly. "It's almost better than going into town to a restaurant. And I insist that you eat dinner with us tomorrow night." She looked at Byron fondly as she walked into the kitchen. "How are you, Junior?"

"Just fine. And you look lovely," Byron replied, causing the old woman's face to glow.

China noticed that Karly had changed into a fresh dress—and one of her better ones, at that. She glanced back at her husband with a knowing smile, as if to say, "I told you he would notice," and China smiled at Byron. He was a charmer all right.

Randolph walked over and shook Byron's hand. "How are you, Junior? It's so good of you to let us share this meal with you."

"We wouldn't have missed it for all the world," Byron said. He glanced at China slyly, and she had to smile at him. He surprised her by leaving the candles on the table. She had expected him to remove the romantic trappings.

"Well, come on and sit down," he said graciously. "Everything is waiting."

China, Karly, and Randolph sat down, and when Byron had lit the candles, he turned off the kitchen light.

"Well, I declare, isn't this just so romantic?" Karly asked. "I feel as excited as a young bride. And Junior did it all himself. The girl that gets him will get a real prize, won't she?"

She glanced at China, who looked away, praying that the old couple were not going to start matchmaking. "There's nothing romantic about those candles," China said. "Byron just doesn't want you to see what you're eating."

Much to her relief, everyone laughed, and soon Byron had the couple engaged in conversation of a different nature, talking about colorful locals who had lived in the area for a long time.

The evening passed quickly for China, who was much too aware of Byron sitting across the table from her. He was indeed charming—too charming, in fact—and therein lay the danger. He was wonderful with the old people. He had been acquainted with them for so many years that he knew them almost as well as China did, perhaps better, for he had obviously spent more time with them.

Finally he turned on the lights to put on a pot of coffee water. "Oh, no," Karly cried. "I forgot the cinnamon rolls." She looked at Randolph. "Will you go and get them for me? They're on the kitchen table."

Byron shook his head. "Nonsense, Karly. As much as I love your cinnamon rolls, I can't let Randolph go back for them. I have something special I've fixed for dessert."

"Oh," Karly said. "Well, only if you promise to let me send Randolph over with the rolls in the morning. You and China can have them for breakfast."

"Fine. That'll be just fine," Byron said, winking at China.

She glanced away. The thought of having breakfast with him in the morning suddenly seemed incredibly intimate. She was glad when she heard the water start to boil in the pot. "I'll make the coffee," she said.

"Good," Byron said. "I'll serve the dessert." He went to the stove and, with a flourish, uncovered a dish.

"Coconut flan," he said, not very modestly.

"I love it," China admitted, duly impressed. She realized that he had gone to no small trouble in preparing this meal.

104

When he had served up individual portions, he took them to the table. China soon followed with coffee. The four of them ate the treat and chatted awhile longer. Then Karly looked at Randolph meaningfully.

"We'd really better be getting back. Junior's been busy all evening, cooking, and he probably should be in bed."

Byron looked at China. "So you told them of your crime."

She laughed. "Yes, I confessed."

"Really," he said, "despite the fact that she tried to kill me, I'm quite all right. I was stunned there for a while, but I've made a miraculous recovery." He glanced at China. "Of course, I still don't know if my virtue was compromised. Did she also tell you that she completely undressed me?"

China saw that he had hoped to shock her with that little revelation, and she was glad she had beaten him to the punch.

"Yes, she told us," Karly said, smiling. "You two young folks seem to be having quite a time over here."

"Not nearly the time we're planning to have," Byron said mischievously.

China glared at him, but he didn't bat an eye.

"Well, in that case, I guess we had best be on our way," Randolph said, standing up.

"Don't you dare hurry off just because Junior's having a little fun," China insisted, suddenly wanting them to stay more than ever. "Why don't we get up a hand of cards? It'll be us girls against you fellows."

The old man glanced at his wife hopefully, but he saw that it was a lost cause. Karly wanted to leave the two young people alone. "Maybe later in the week," he said resignedly. "It's late. Us old folks have to get to bed."

"That sounds like a good idea for us young folks too," Byron said wickedly, grinning at China.

"I don't go to bed this early," she said emphatically. She did not want the guests to think there was any reason for Byron's broad hints. "You can do as you please, and I think bed is a good idea for you. Your brain is still muddled from the bashing I gave you."

Tossing back his blond head, Byron laughed heartily; when

Randolph joined in, China glared from one to the other. She didn't think Byron was funny at all now.

"Come on, Randolph," Karly insisted. "We'd best be on our way."

"I'll see you to the door," China said. She left with the couple, and when she looked over her shoulder, she saw that Byron was right behind her. China turned on the porch light and followed Karly and Randolph outside. She waited until they were down the steps and moving toward the trees before she turned back to Byron.

"Just what were you trying to make them think?" she demanded. "It sounded like we were already sleeping together."

"*Already?*" he teased. "Why, China, what a splendid idea. Let's try it." He drew her back against his hard body, but China spun out of his arms.

"Stop that."

He laughed gently. "Come on back inside and help me with the dishes."

She did go back inside, but she didn't intend to help him. She wanted to get as far away from him as possible. "I'll do them, since you cooked. Why don't you go to bed? Really, you know you did suffer quite an injury to your head. I'm sure you need to rest."

"Only if you'll lie down with me," he said, a gleam in his gray eyes.

"Don't be silly," China chided. "I'm not going to do that."

"Alas," Byron said, as if utterly disappointed, "I guess there's nothing to do but help you with the dishes, then."

"I don't need your help. I'd rather do them by myself."

"But I'm the housewife here," Byron reminded her.

China turned away from him; clearly she was no match for him. She went to the table and began to gather up the dishes, and when she returned to the sink with them, she found that Byron was already running the water. There was nothing to do but get this over with.

They had finished in a short time, and China watched suspiciously as Byron took the wine out of the refrigerator. "Now," he said, "surely you'll have a little nightcap with me."

Sighing wearily, she nodded. She was wound up tighter than

106

a drum. The meal had been special despite her heightened awareness of Byron, and a few tense moments. She had immensely enjoyed the time with her dinner companions, but now that she had Byron all to herself, she suddenly didn't know what to do or say. Perhaps the wine would relax her.

"I'll start a fire in the living room," he said.

"Oh, dear," China muttered.

Looking at her in amusement, Byron asked, "What's wrong?"

"I beg your pardon?"

"You said 'Oh, dear' and I wondered what was wrong," Byron said.

Damn him, China thought, he knew what was wrong; he was making her a nervous wreck. "Oh, nothing," she said. "I was just muttering again."

"I know. I heard."

"If you'll excuse me," she said, turning away, "I've got to cover Blue for the night. He'll think I've forgotten him."

"Well, hurry back to the living room or I'll think you've forgotten me," Byron murmured.

"Impossible," China muttered under her breath. "Absolutely impossible." But she hoped Byron hadn't heard what she had said this time.

She dallied in her room, killing time, getting up the nerve to go to the living room, for she was sure she knew what to expect when she got there. Finally she covered Blue, then left the room. When she joined Byron, she wasn't surprised to find that he had built a roaring fire in the fireplace and turned the lamp to its lowest setting. He had settled down on the couch and was comfortably sipping a glass of white wine.

"Ah, there you are," he said, patting a spot on the couch beside him. "Come join me."

China felt like sitting all the way across the room from him, but she didn't want him to know how afraid she was of her own ability to resist him. She sat down on the couch some distance from him, but he wasn't deterred in the slightest.

"Here, let me pour some wine for you," he offered. When he had done so, he moved down next to her, so close that she could feel the heat from his body.

107

Oh, Lord, she told herself, what was she doing here with this barracuda? The water was way too deep and she didn't swim well.

She accepted the glass of wine and sipped it nervously. Byron was smiling and making small talk, asking her how she had liked the meal he had cooked and what she thought of Karly and Randolph. Before China knew it, she had finished the contents of her glass and Byron had refilled it.

He moved closer to her until his leg was touching hers, and China trembled uncontrollably as fire burned through her veins.

"Cold?" he asked solicitously. Before she could say no, he had set his glass of wine down and wrapped his arms around her shoulders.

"Really, that won't be necessary," she said crisply, her heart beating wildly.

"No?" he said in a low voice. "Well, this will be." He turned her chin with his index finger, and before she could draw away, his mouth closed over hers.

China had known all evening that it would come to this, and although she had subconsciously prepared herself to resist, she found that she was helpless to do so now. She realized with a shiver of disbelief that she hungered for this man's kisses. Never had she wanted a man more—not even Dereck.

Byron's mouth moved tantalizingly against hers, and China found herself returning the heat in his kiss. His hands roamed seductively over her back and shoulders, and she could feel the warmth of his fingers, even through her heavy sweater.

"I don't really think you need this with that fire," he murmured, helping her slide the garment off. China watched as he laid it on the back of the couch, then reached out for her. When his hands touched her bare skin, she shivered again. Byron's lips left hers to scatter teasing kisses down the length of her neck, and soon his fingers had found the tiny buttons on the front of her dress. She knew she had to stop him before this got out of hand; she had no intention in the world of becoming the next in line on this couch after Marlene, but he was so damned exciting.

He easily undid the buttons and began to take small love bites of the pale flesh spilling over the lacy bra covering her breasts.

108

China locked her fingers in his blond curls and closed her eyes as thrill after thrill raced over her skin. Byron's hands moved hotly over her breasts, finding the stiff peaks, titillating them as no other man had ever done.

She opened her mouth to protest when he undid the front hook of her bra, exposing her breasts completely to his hands and mouth, but when his tongue found one of her nipples and licked it tantalizingly, China's good intentions were lost in a flood of erotic sensations.

Byron's thumb and finger caressed one nipple while his tongue teased the other, and China found herself succumbing to his heady seduction, her body betraying her mind. When his mouth found hers again, she knew that she had lost the battle against her own doubts. Byron's hands slid under the skirt of her dress to stroke her satin thighs sensually, and her flesh burned everywhere he touched it. She longed to know the ultimate power of his fire. She could feel the fever inside her racing out of control, and she yearned to have him quench the roaring blazes.

Byron eased her nylons down her long legs, kissing her quivering flesh en route. Then he slid her lacy half-slip off and flung it aside. Suddenly there was a loud crash as it landed against the bottle of wine. The bottle toppled over, spilling its contents down one of China's legs.

Abruptly she began to laugh, more from relief than any other reason. She and Byron Scott would make a good comedy team, she told herself.

But this particular incident had saved her, and she was going to take advantage of it. "I'll clean up this mess," she said, hurriedly rebuttoning her dress, then switching the lamp on to its brightest intensity.

"Never mind," Byron muttered. "I made the mess; I'll clean it up."

Grateful for a chance to escape, China smiled faintly at him as she stood up. "Well, then, I'll wish you a good night, Byron." Then she fled down the hall to her bedroom.

When she was safely inside, she told herself that she had had a narrow escape. But to her dismay she wasn't sure now that she had wanted to be saved. The blazes that had been so coldly

and suddenly dampened by the spilled wine were now smoldering embers, and as China stripped off her clothes she found that
her body was still throbbing in anticipation of satisfaction that
would not come.

"Oh, damn," she muttered. "What am I doing here? Why am
I doing this to myself?" But there was no answer to her question, only the lonely silence filling the room.

China had rushed away too quickly, leaving a frustrated Byron behind to shake his head at his own bungling of the evening. "Good show, ol' boy," he muttered aloud. "You're doing
real well. Why, if I didn't know better, I'd say you were behaving like a damned kid in love."

His words startled him, and for a moment he fell silent as he
watched the last drops of the wine trickle down on the floor in
front of the couch.

Then a smile curved his lips. Just two days earlier he had
thought the funniest thing he had ever heard was that story
about Blue being sexually frustrated. Now he'd be damned if he
wasn't beginning to empathize with him. Tonight he was feeling
like they were birds of a feather. He tossed back his blond head
and laughed aloud.

"Dammit, Colleen," he muttered, "you'd better not be up
there somewhere, laughing your head off at me."

CHAPTER EIGHT

The next morning China awakened early despite her restless
night. She felt sure that she had gotten up before Byron, but
when she stumbled down the hall to the bathroom, she heard
him in the kitchen, talking to Demon.

She smiled a little to herself. He wasn't so unlike her, after
all. The first thing she did in the morning was talk to Blue. She

hadn't yet uncovered him, but as soon as she cleaned up, she would.

She glanced down at the sexy deep-blue nightgown and matching robe she wore. Another outfit from her trousseau. She thought of Dereck, amazed that she could recall his name after that to-do with Byron last night. With a tremor of remembered warmth she recalled that, had it not been for his clumsiness, he would be the one seeing this gown now.

A smile played on her full lips. And then again, maybe he wouldn't. She doubted that his women wore much of anything. His *women,* she reminded herself distastefully. The last thing she wanted to be was *one* of his women.

She found herself staying much too long in the bathroom, brushing her hair, putting on lipstick. She didn't have to ask herself whom she was trying to impress, and it annoyed her terribly. She made herself stop putting on makeup, having settled for lipstick and a little powder over her ivory skin.

When she had returned to her room, she uncovered Blue, who started right in with his phrase for the day: "You're young, you'll get over it."

"Thanks a lot," China muttered.

"Thanks a lot," he repeated as she carried his cage down the hall.

China pushed against   kitchen door. She could smell coffee, and she was dying for a cup, but should she dare take Blue into the same room with Demon? "Hello?" she said tentatively, peering into the room.

Byron smiled at her as he gave her an appreciative glance that told her the exotic outfit wasn't wasted. He was sitting at the table with Demon on his lap. "Good morning. Come on in. I have the decadent monster on my lap, where he can do little damage."

China laughed lightly as she walked inside and suspended Blue's cage from a hook on the ceiling. She wondered why she hadn't thought of it before. Even Demon wasn't adept at climbing the walls, she told herself, glancing askance at him as if to be sure.

"The water's still hot. Have a cup of coffee with me," Byron suggested.

111

"Sounds good," China murmured. "I wish Randolph would come over with those cinnamon rolls. I'm hungry."

No sooner had she said the words than a knock sounded at the back door. "Speak of the devil . . ." she murmured, using one of Granny's old phrases.

When she went to the back door, Randolph was there, a plate of warm buttered rolls in hand. "Well, good morning," China said brightly. "Come on in."

He shook his head. "No, thank you. I have strict orders to leave the rolls and get back to the house." He glanced up at the sky. "Looks like the rain's finally stopped, and Karly has a dozen chores for me today."

China grinned at him. Karly did believe in keeping him busy. She always said confidentially that it kept him from getting old. "Thank you so much for these," she said, taking the plate. "I was just telling Byron that I wished you would bring them."

"I'm a mind reader, I reckon. Either that, or Karly is. She's the one who sent me."

"You have a nice day, Randolph, and you and Karly come on over later and let's play some cards."

"We'll see," the old man said, shrugging, as if he knew it were hopeless. "We'll see."

China watched as he made his way down the steps, then went back to the kitchen.

"Manna from heaven," Byron exclaimed dramatically, looking upward.

"Rolls from Karly," China said truthfully, but she grinned at him as she set the plate down.

"Can I fix you a cup of coffee?" he asked. "I'm going to get another one." Standing up, he cradled Demon in one arm.

China nodded as she began to bite into one of the delicious rolls. "Yes, please."

When Byron had taken Demon to the library and made fresh cups of coffee, he returned to the table. "I have to go attempt to get my car out of the mud," he said. "I don't suppose you would be willing to lend me a hand."

Yes, indeed, she would, she told herself swiftly. If he could get his car back on the road, maybe he, too, would be back on the road and out of her life before something drastic happened.

112

The thought suddenly unsettled her, but that only reinforced her desire to have him leave as quickly as possible.

"Of course," she said casually. "You would do the same for me, wouldn't you?"

Byron smiled, and China wasn't sure what to make of it until he murmured, "Think you'll be rid of me if the car is mobile, do you?"

"My word, am I that transparent?" China muttered, looking at him with wide eyes.

Byron's gaze swept over her again, lingering on her curves in the slinky nightwear. "Almost but not quite. In fact, I'd like to see a little more transparency."

"You know that's not what I was talking about," she said emphatically.

"No?" he murmured low. "You do wear those gowns to tantalize me, don't you?"

"No," she retorted. "They're all I have."

His gray eyes whipped over her again. "And I'm delighted—truly I am. You do dress in style. In fact, I've never known a woman who would come to a cabin all alone and get so dolled up. Someone must have paid a fortune for them."

Staring down at her steaming cup of coffee, China muttered, "I don't *always* dress like this. These gowns were for my honeymoon. They are all I packed, so I decided to enjoy them myself." Her eyes met his defiantly. "And someone did pay a fortune for them: *I* did. I got them at the shops I manage. I get an employee discount, and I love pretty things just like any other woman. Heaven knows, I work hard for them."

"Now, what can be hard about working in a dress shop?" Byron asked.

"Are you serious? You work with the public; you know they can be impossible if they want to. And it seems that the richer they are, the more impossible they try to be." She shrugged. "And the hours! I hardly ever get two days off in a row, and just when I do think I have them, something comes up that ties me to one of the stores. Still, this is the work I love. It's what I chose. I studied dress design, but I found that I enjoyed working with people more than with pen and paper." Shaking her head, she added, "It seems ironic that many of my days are spent at a desk, doing book work and ordering clothes."

Byron looked at her thoughtfully as she sat there, daring him to comment. So, he told himself, he had been wrong again. She took her work, and herself, very seriously. And she had made it all too plain that no one lavished beautiful clothes on her. She even had a viable excuse for not coming to see her granny often. How could she make the trip in a day?

He smiled. He had intended to tell her that she could have dressed in street clothes instead of strutting around in front of him in those sexy gowns, but now he couldn't say it. "Well, I'm glad you wore your gowns. They're stunning, and so are you."

"You're young, you'll get over it," Blue chimed in, causing Byron to laugh softly.

"Clever bird," he said, "but I don't think you'll get over it anytime soon."

China wanted to tell him not to bother to flatter her, but she was too pleased by his compliment to bicker about it. Wasn't that part of the reason she had been wearing such gorgeous, provocative gowns in front of him? Wasn't she still trying to get him to notice her? To think she was attractive? After all, she could have dressed in something else before she left her room.

Rejection in any form wasn't easy for her to take; it had been a painful experience, finding out that Dereck was still interested in other women. She didn't need Byron Scott to come along right after that and tell her he didn't find her appealing.

She smiled grimly to herself. She didn't know how she had ever gotten mixed up with Dereck in the first place. Physical attraction, she guessed, and then that thing called love. Well, she hoped she had learned her lesson. He had been her first failure in life—and what a big one!

"So you'll go with me to try and move the car?" Byron said, breaking into her thoughts.

She nodded. "I told you I would."

"Well, I can think of a place or two where I'd like to take you dressed like that," Byron said, his eyes dark and suggestive, "but if we're going to dig my car out of the mud, maybe you should change clothes."

She wanted to tell him that of course she wasn't going

114

dressed like this, but she realized that it was absurd. He was only teasing, and she was too busy being flattered by his comments to think rationally.

"I won't be long," she said, getting up. She took her coffee cup to the sink and washed it, then removed Blue's cage from the hook. She could feel Byron's gaze on her and didn't turn around.

"Thanks a lot," Blue squawked, eyeing Byron as they left the room.

"You don't have to thank him for anything," China muttered under her breath. She was grateful that she and Byron weren't going to be shut up in this house together all day, and if she was lucky, he would soon be on his way to somewhere else.

She chose the only appropriate clothes she had with her, her jeans and a blue sweater. She also had a pair of tennis shoes— not really appropriate, but the closest thing she could find. She dressed in a matter of minutes, and with her jacket slung over her arm she returned to the kitchen.

Byron was staring out the window, watching the sea crash against the ragged shoreline.

"I love it here," he said without turning around. "Sometimes I wish I could just stay here and forget all that restaurant business."

That surprised China. She had told herself the same kind of thing dozens of times. "I know what you mean," she said pensively. "If I were rich . . ."

She let the words trail off when Byron turned around and regarded her questioningly. "If I were rich," he said, grinning, "I'd do anything I please." He shook his head. "That's not true, you know. It's too easy just to sit back and let the profits increase while someone else does the work. A man needs to keep biting into life, to let himself know he's alive."

"That's your theory," China said, shrugging it off. But she knew exactly what he was talking about. When Gramps and Granny had lived here all those years, they had worked hard with their cattle. They hadn't just lain back and let the rest of the world run on by.

"I'm ready when you are," Byron said. "I'm not real sure where I left the car. It was so dark and the rain was pouring. I

115

turned off the main highway onto the dirt road, and I passed several houses, so I think I left it about a mile down the road."

"Can you walk that far?" China teased. "A city boy like you?"

"I'll bet I can manage better than you."

"I doubt it," she flung back at him.

They stepped outside to find a cool but sunny day. It was marvelous to see the sun again, but it would be some time before the earth dried out. Water stood in puddles everywhere, and China could just imagine the condition Byron's car would be in after sitting on the muddy road for a couple of nights.

"Are there some boards around that we can use for leverage to free the back tires?" he asked.

She wasn't sure. "Maybe in the shed around back," she suggested, and when they went there, they found what Byron seemed to want. He also took a shovel with him.

China couldn't help but smile to herself. Instinctively she knew this was going to prove entertaining.

With two short boards and the shovel under one arm, Byron set out to rescue his car. He and China walked quietly for some time, enjoying the solitude and the fresh air, which was still filled with the damp smell of rain. The road was slick and sprinkled with ruts and potholes. China didn't resist when Byron locked her arm in his, but she could feel the erratic beating of her heart at the unexpected contact.

At last they spied the car at the end of the dirt road leading directly to the Castleberry land. China could see that it would be no easy task to get it out. Clearly, Byron had spun the tires until they had dug graves for themselves, and the rain that had fallen afterward had only made the situation worse.

"We should have just called a tow truck," she told him.

To her surprise he laughed. "You're probably right, but why should I pay some other guy when I can do it myself?"

She saw immediately that it wasn't the money that was at issue with this man; he loved the challenge! But that silver Rolls-Royce stuck in the mud didn't quite seem like his cup of tea. It seemed ludicrous to her that this wealthy, polished blond man was going to play around in the mud to free his expensive car.

116

She smiled at him as she watched him assess the situation, then put a board under one of the back tires. China took the other board and gingerly worked her way to the other side of the car, where, with some maneuvering, she managed to get her board positioned in front of the other rear tire.

Byron was watching her, and he smiled as she straightened up. Her hands were already filthy, but then, so were his. He laughed lightly at the sight they presented, and China joined in.

"Well, we'll see what happens," Byron said. "Now, stand back a little. I'm going to start the engine."

China stepped off to the side, burying her hands in her pockets as she waited to see if the car would start. Finally it caught, and the smooth engine purred to life. To her horror she found that she was standing right in the path of the mud that flew up from one of the back wheels! It coated her from her hair and face down to her hips.

"Oh, dammit," she sputtered, wiping at the gooey mess that clung to her face.

Byron, looking at her in the rearview mirror for some sign of success or failure, began to laugh at the sight. He was still laughing loudly when he stepped out of the car and approached her.

"Think it's funny, do you?" she blurted, and before Byron knew what was happening, China stuck one foot out and tripped him.

She broke into laughter as he tumbled forward. He tried to stop the fall with his hands, but they slid out from under him, and he landed facedown on the muddy road.

He looked up at her once, then folded his arms one over the other and let his head drop down on them. China laughed again, thinking he was just teasing, but when he didn't move a muscle, her hands flew to her mouth.

Good heavens, what had she been thinking? He had just suffered a head injury: Maybe the fall had aggravated it and he had actually passed out.

Her lips trembling, she bent down over his prostrate form. "Byron," she whispered, tears filling her eyes. "Oh, God, Byron, are you all right?"

Suddenly he turned, grabbed her, and pulled her down into the mud with him, laughing uproariously.

"You damned, crazy fool!" she roared. "You frightened me half to death."

"Good," he said. "That proves you care."

China couldn't believe they were wallowing in the mud like pigs, but that wasn't the half of it. Still chuckling, Byron gazed at her for a moment, then rolled over on his back and drew her down to kiss her.

China could feel his muscular body, even through the mud-splattered layers of clothing that separated them, and felt the excitement build inside her as his lips moved warmly against hers. His tongue explored the velvety interior of her mouth; it entwined sensually with hers, tasting and touching, creating new flames of desire inside her.

Byron's hands moved possessively over China's back and hips, and she thrilled to his touch. It took all her willpower to remember that they were on a dirt road instead of in a Garden of Eden. She told herself that she should make some token protest, but it wasn't until Byron's lips freed hers that she was able to think of anything at all to say.

When she could catch her breath, she cried, "Byron, for heaven's sake, let's get up off the road."

"Where do you want to go to continue this?" he teased.

Shaking her head at his persistence, she pulled away from him and managed to stand up. She was a sight, but so was he. His entire front and back were covered with mud, and China couldn't help but laugh when he stood up. There was no way to brush the mess off.

Byron winked at her. "You're kind of cute yourself, Che-Che," he said.

Che-Che was just what she felt like—a little girl playing in the mud. "Wait until you get a glimpse of yourself, Junior," she joked.

"Well, come on," he said. "Let's try again. The boards didn't quite do it, did they? I'm going to have to dig some of the mud away from the tires."

China stepped way back this time while he worked, but she couldn't stop smiling. The man was crazy. No wonder Granny had been so taken with him. He might have been angry that China had tripped him, but instead he had laughed good-naturedly and tried to turn the situation to his advantage. One thing she had to admit: He was a good sport. He was so relaxed that it almost seemed as if he were unaware of the power his money gave him. She couldn't think of another man she knew who could easily pay someone else to do this who would be out here sweating and sloshing around in the mud.

After several minutes of concentrated effort, Byron called, "This time we'll do it!" He repositioned the boards, then found some leafy branches to give the tires more traction. Smiling at his optimism, China stepped back away from the car—this time far away.

It took a bit of work, but at last the sleek silver car pulled free of the pit that had held it. Byron got out, grinning triumphantly.

"Hooray!" China shouted. "Hooray!"

Byron was beaming like a little boy, as though he had really accomplished some incredible feat, and both of them laughed as China climbed into the car.

"Oh, damn," she muttered, moving her leg back out. "I forgot about the upholstery. I can't sit in here covered with mud."

"Get in," he said. "You're not as bad as I am, and I've already done it. It'll clean—and cost less than the man coming out from Monterey would charge to pull the car out of the mud."

China sat down, but she was uncomfortable. "Don't you have road service that would have paid for this?" she asked.

He nodded. "Hell, yes, but wasn't this fun?"

"You're crazy, man," she said. "Crazy."

He just chuckled softly to himself, then drove back to the cabin. "I'll race you to the shower," he said when they had gotten out of the car.

"You're on," she cried. She couldn't remember when she had behaved like such a fool, but she didn't intend to worry about it. Byron was clearly enjoying himself immensely. He was so different from the blond stranger she had met that first night; right now she thought he was really delightful. And she didn't want the laughter to stop.

119

She reached the shower first, perhaps because she was more determined. "You lose," she called over her shoulder.

"Don't be so sure," he said from the other side of the door as she shut it behind her and began to strip off her clothes.

China paused for a moment, wondering what he had meant by that, but the thought of the hot water flooding down over her, cleaning off the grime and warming her, was so enticing that she didn't linger for long. She quickly caught her dark hair up on her head with a clasp, turned on the spray, adjusted it to the right temperature, then stepped inside.

She was glorying in the delicious feel of the water cascading down over her body when she heard the shower door open again. She turned to peer through the water.

"Byron!" she cried, as he joined her, his long, lean body as naked as hers. *"What do you think you're doing?"*

He grinned innocently. "Why, anybody can see what I'm doing. I'm taking a shower with you."

"Oh, no you're not," she sputtered, trying to look anywhere but at his handsome, hairy body.

He wasn't having the same trouble she was. His gray eyes relished the sight of her tall, shapely frame; he couldn't seem to look anywhere else. "China, you are one beautiful woman," he murmured thickly. "So very beautiful. I've dreamed of you, and I've touched you, and I still can't get over your beauty."

"Now, you just get right out of here!" she ordered, her voice rising.

"Shh," he said gently. "Stop that talk." Then he turned her around and drew her to him, molding his long, hard body to hers.

China told herself vehemently that the last thing she needed was to become involved with a man like Byron. She had learned her lesson and learned it well. She had no intention of making that mistake again. She pushed against his chest with her palms. "No, Byron," she said firmly.

But Byron wasn't a man easily deterred. He gazed steadily into her dark eyes. "Yes, China," he murmured. "We're made for each other and you know it. Your granny knew it. I want you."

His gray eyes glowed with desire, and when his mouth sought

hers, China uttered a weak protest against his lips. She wanted desperately to turn away, but his touch excited her too much. His hips were still pressed intimately to hers, and she was much too aware of just how much he did want her. He was so virile and so intoxicating and so close that he seemed to burn right into her body. He confused her logical mind by arousing her physically; her signals became all muddled by his magnetic appeal.

He drew her nearer despite her hands pushing against his chest, and she was acutely aware of the potent male power of him. Her resistance to him was already shaky, and she gradually yielded to the excitement surging inside her. Her fingers slid around his chest to his back, and she drew him more tightly to her curves.

He began to scatter feather-light kisses over her face, calming her fears and quieting any doubts that still hovered. Then he took her mouth in passionate possession, his lips moving firmly against hers, and she melted into his embrace.

The water rushed down over them as they kissed, their tongues meeting in a dance of desire. Byron's mouth moved thrillingly against China's, and she could feel the savage beating of her heart as it echoed the pounding of his.

His fingers began an erotic, sensual massage of her face, outlining her features with a gentle touch before they moved down her neck to stroke the smooth white column with a sensitive caress.

Then his hands moved enticingly over her naked curves, exploring and burning, hungrily touching each part of her, stoking the blazes that had begun to roar hotly inside her. Her fingers stroked his hard back, tracing the firm contours, and she felt her nipples tingle as they hardened against the curling hair of Byron's chest. His hips were pressed tightly to hers, and she could feel his manhood burning against her, inciting flames of passion in her most feminine depths.

His mouth left hers to trail hot kisses down the wet skin of her throat, and she arched her neck, wanting more and still more. Her veins were running with wildfire, and every caress of Byron's hands and lips fueled the flames until she thought she couldn't stand it anymore.

121

Byron's tongue trailed around her damp throat, then lower, and he licked at the thrusting nipples of first one breast, then the other. China heard herself moan softly as the fire blazed higher and higher inside her.

She found herself eager to know each line and angle of Byron's exciting body. She felt as if she were drowning in the wild sensations he was creating inside her. Her blood was at the boiling point, and a fever raged in her like none she had ever imagined.

When Byron's mouth returned to claim her lips again, China gripped his blond curls tightly. She could feel the full length of his body now as he molded himself to her, his bold masculinity a provocative invitation she couldn't resist. He began to move his hips slightly against hers, rocking gently, sending rivers of fire rushing up her body.

She felt a deep, hungry need within her, and she yearned to know the full power of his potent arousal. His fingers were tracing her curves again, following the silhouette of her breasts, and she moaned softly when his palms made tantalizing circles over the sensitive nipples. Her mouth parted automatically, and Byron teased her with his kisses and his tongue, causing the fires to burn out of control inside her. She gasped when he began to explore the heart of her passion, and she sucked in her breath when he eased his manhood inside her, becoming one with her for the first time.

"Oh, Byron," she murmured.

"You feel so good, China," he whispered huskily, his breath warm on her skin. "So good."

His gray gaze held hers, hypnotizing her, daring her to close her eyes or look away. She felt as if he had thrown a web of love over her, making her the willing captive of his passion and her own, and she relished each imaginary glistening gold strand that represented his hold on her. His eyes glittered with a reflection of her own desires, and China gave him a slow, mysterious smile as she was drawn into the ecstasy of the moment.

He began to move slowly, erotically, his thrusts long and deep as he pressed her rounded hips against the powerful lines of his. China felt herself sinking further and further into the vortex of passion, whirling toward a never-never land where mind and body touched in the ultimate union.

Byron began to move faster, gradually increasing the pace of their love dance, and China's fingers dug into his muscled back. She had never known that making love could be so total, so complete, that she wanted to leave the here and now behind for the pleasures of the senses. The desire she was experiencing had muted reality, but the rapture she felt was all too real.

At last Byron arched his body against hers a final time, and China let her teeth close down gently on the flesh of his shoulder as she received him. For a brief eternity she rode away on the wings of desire, caught up in an incredible kaleidoscope of exquisite mental and physical sensations she had never before experienced. If this was how it was meant to be, she didn't ever want to step back into the real world.

Nevertheless, soon she began to ease back down to earth. Byron was still joined with her, holding her body to his. She looked into his glazed eyes and saw her own ecstasy mirrored there.

"Oh, Che-Che," he murmured thickly, "to think that all those years I avoided meeting Colleen's little granddaughter. Woman, you are really something special. I had no idea."

China smiled, suddenly shy, now that the haze of desire had begun to fade. For a moment she felt a little ashamed of herself. This wasn't what Granny had had in mind, she knew, but she couldn't deny that it had been wonderful. Byron had been wonderful. The loving had been exquisite. But she would be a fool to think that there was anything more to it than that.

Sensing her withdrawal, Byron freed her and turned to shut off the water. China reached out for a towel, and when Byron offered to dry her, she shook her head.

Watching her, Byron knew that she was slipping away from him, but he didn't know what to do about it. He wasn't going to speak meaningless words to her or promise her anything for the future, but he knew that China was feeling uncomfortable about having made love with him. He had hoped that she had found the experience as wondrous as he. And he sensed that she had.

He watched her as she dried off and stepped out of the shower, and when she freed her long, dark hair from the clasp and shook it out, he told himself she was the most gorgeous creature he had ever seen.

She didn't say anything as she left the bathroom, and he became pensive as he reached for a towel and dried himself. China wasn't like the other women in his life, and he hadn't expected her to be. She was troubled now—but why? Was it because they had made love?

Or was it Dereck? She could be feeling one of two emotions now, and Byron wasn't pleased about either: She could be wondering how she could give herself to another man so completely if she had really loved Dereck, or she could be justifying the act in her mind as a way of putting Dereck behind her and going on with life.

He sighed, suddenly finding the magic moments of the loving vanishing in his scrutiny of the reasons behind it. Maybe he shouldn't have taken her, but he hadn't been able to resist. He had wanted her so badly that he had ached for her.

"Oh, hell," he grumbled unhappily. What now? How would she behave toward him now that the budding friendship had been suddenly catapulted into a sexually explosive union?

He stepped out into the hall and found his muddy clothes where he had left them. He hadn't taken the time to get his luggage out of the car; he had been in too much of a hurry to join China in the shower, and now he had to put those dirty garments back on while he went to retrieve his suitcase.

But he was glad to have something to do. China was still in her room, and he didn't have the heart to knock on the door. This was his first experience of this kind, and for once in his life he didn't know how to handle a woman. Had he just made love to anyone else, he would be right back with her, nuzzling and whispering love words, thinking of the pleasure they had shared. But with China—hell, he didn't know what he was doing.

Suddenly he looked at the ceiling. "Dammit, Colleen, you've put me in a hell of a mess. I don't know if I'm coming or going."

When he had gotten his suitcase from the car, he went into his room and changed his clothes. Then, feeling lost, he glanced at China's closed door once before he went to the library and got Demon.

He saw China going toward the kitchen as he walked out of the room, and when he followed he was just in time to see the back door close behind her. His first instinct was to put Demon down and run after her. They needed to talk, but about what? What would he say to her?

"Ah, hell," he muttered again. What was he doing here? Why had he gone and complicated his life by making love to her? He went into the living room with Demon and slumped disconsolately onto the couch. Why was his life suddenly so complex? A week earlier he had meant to come here only to get some rest after the opening of his newest restaurant. Now he found himself unexpectedly involved in China Castleberry's life. How the hell had that happened? And why did the thought bother him so much?

CHAPTER NINE

China's tennis shoes became soaked as she walked through the wet woods, staring down at the broken branches and fallen leaves. Instead of finding peace of mind at Big Sur, she had only added to her problems. She wanted to blame someone, like Granny, for her troubles, but Granny hadn't made her make love with Byron Scott. She had done that all on her own, much too willingly.

"Oh, China," she chastised herself, "do you like punishment? You can't be that big a fool, can you? The man is just like Dereck. Why did you make love with him? Do you want to get caught up in another situation like the one you just got out of only days ago?" she wondered, feeling a rush of guilt that she could go into another man's arms so soon after breaking up with Dereck.

She shook her head and tried very hard to downplay the importance of the act. She and Byron had made love. So what? That certainly didn't mean she was going to have a relationship with him like the one she had had with Dereck. In fact, she realized with a surge of alarm, it didn't mean that they would have a relationship at all.

That realization bothered her most of all. She knew how Byron felt about that kind of thing, and she certainly knew what he thought about marriage. He had made his position perfectly clear.

For a while longer she walked through the woods, oblivious to the beauty all around her, muttering to herself. She could reason and make logical explanations all night and all day, but if she didn't want something more from Byron than a single day's lovemaking, she never would have gone into his arms. She could tell her mind anything, but her heart didn't even hear her idle words.

She couldn't believe it: Byron wasn't just a passing stranger who happened to own half her house. No, he was more than that. But she didn't want to think about just how much more.

Byron was still sitting on the couch an hour later when China returned. He looked up expectantly when she walked into the room. She had picked up Blue and was talking to the bird as though he and she were the only occupants of the house.

"Hello, pretty baby," she murmured. Then she kissed his beak.

"Kiss, kiss," Blue called softly.

"That's a damned good idea," Byron muttered under his breath, but China gave no indication that she had heard him.

"China," he said in a low voice, "come over here and sit by me." He patted the couch cushion beside him, but when China looked back over her shoulder at him, he saw the tension in her features. She gave him a faint smile, then put Blue on his perch.

"Kiss, kiss," Blue called out, and China briefly kissed his beak again. He began to make buzzing sounds deep in his throat, and Byron smiled. That damned bird got more attention than he did.

When China had joined him on the couch, he took her hand and held it to his lips. "Blue has the right idea," he said. "You're a woman who should be kissed—and often."

"Shouldn't any woman?" she asked, forcing a smile.

Byron shook his head. "No, not any woman."

China looked away. She didn't want to start reading something into his innocent banter. She didn't want to get hurt again.

Byron sensed her discomfort around him, and it bothered him much more than he had expected it to. He didn't want her to be unhappy, and he realized suddenly that her happiness was very important to him.

"China, are you sorry we made love?" he asked gently.

Her dark gaze flew to his. "No, of course not," she said with feigned lightness. "I had a great time, didn't you?"

But Byron, watching her through thoughtful gray eyes, saw through her facade. She was as easy to read as a book; when she got upset, those dark eyes reflected her inner turmoil, and her ivory skin became even whiter. Her sweet smile trembled on her lips. She *was* sorry, and he saw that it would be very difficult for him to cultivate a relationship with her as long as they were cooped up in this cabin. He didn't want to remain here with her where she had to fight her memories of Granny and Dereck.

What she needed was an entire change of pace so that she could clear her head and get her life back on course. Byron was sorry now that he had come into her life like this, at this time. There had to be some way to make things easier for them both.

Suddenly he remembered her saying how much she had wanted to go to Scotland. His grandparents lived there, and that would work out perfectly. An idea began to grow in his mind; he realized that his only hope to win China's affection was to take her away from here. Perhaps in Scotland it would be possible.

Byron reached out and stroked the dark, silky hair that lay on her shoulders in glossy waves. Then he drew her forward and kissed her mouth. He could sense her hesitation, but soon her mouth softened under the persuasion of his. He wanted her

127

to want him and to be aware that she wanted him when he asked her to go away with him, for he didn't want her to refuse. She began to return his kiss, and he pulled her more tightly to him.

At last he drew away from her. "China," he murmured against her ear, "I want you to go with me to Scotland."

China opened her eyes wide, and for a moment she was so shocked that she just stared at him. Then she cried "What?"

Byron shrugged with a carelessness he did not feel. "Being here, thinking about your grandmother, has made me think of my own grandparents. I've decided I'd like to see them, and since you specifically mentioned that you had planned to go to Scotland, I thought you might like to go with me."

China stared blankly at him. Why was he really asking her? She almost laughed aloud. Surely he wasn't "taking her home to meet the folks." Of course not, she told herself firmly. Byron Scott was used to taking his women anywhere and everywhere with him. Hadn't Marlene proven that? Like the man said, he had decided he wanted to see his grandparents; what was a little trip to Scotland to a wealthy man like him? He had asked as casually as if it mattered very little one way or the other if she went.

She knew she should say no at once. On the other hand . . . China stopped her thoughts from forming. Did she want to flit all over the world with this man as his other women did? Could she be as cavalier about it?

She drew in a steadying breath as she let the question and the possible implications wash over her. She did want to go to Scotland, of course; it was her dream vacation. She couldn't remember when she hadn't wanted to see it. And she would love to do that with someone who had relatives there. What a wonderful opportunity to see a country the way it should be seen instead of following all the usual tourist routes.

By now she knew that Byron would be a marvelous traveling companion. His good nature and his sense of humor would ensure that. And she did want to spend more time with him; there was no use denying it. But to go all that distance with him?

China could feel the tension growing between them, but she

couldn't make a decision like this quickly. Byron was studying her features, and she wondered what he would think if he could read her mind, if he could see how much this mattered to her. She licked her lips. "When are you planning to go?"

Byron took the question as a positive sign, but he knew he wasn't home free yet. "We will have to leave as soon as we can make the arrangements. We don't have much time left before we both have to go back to work."

China nodded. That was all too true. And if she didn't go with Byron, she wouldn't even have this time with him. Maybe she would never see him again. The thought hurt. She stood up and walked over to gaze out the window.

"Give me a few hours to think about it, Byron," she said, but she didn't turn around to look at him. She couldn't. If she did, she was afraid she would agree right away, and she didn't want to make the decision in haste.

She heard his low voice behind her and realized he had come to stand nearby. "I really want you to go with me, China."

A shiver raced over her skin at the husky sound of his voice, but still she didn't turn around. Then she heard him putting some wood on the fire, building it up again. When she turned around, he was gone.

"Thanks a lot," Blue carped, but this time China didn't even hear him. She was too caught up in her own predicament. She turned back to the window, and for a long time she stared out at the churning water, thinking how much it mimicked her own emotions.

It seemed as if she remained in suspended animation for an eternity; then suddenly the old door knocker sounded, startling her. When she went to answer, she saw that Byron had rejoined her in the room and was sitting down on the couch, Demon in his arms.

China realized that she was grateful someone had come— until she opened the door and saw who it was. Her gaze traveled over the tall man, seeing again the dark looks of her fiancé, which were so familiar and once had been so appealing to her. She assessed him from his straight, black hair and ebony eyes, down his broad, muscular body, right to his booted feet, gazing at him as if he were a stranger.

"Hello, China," Dereck said solemnly. "May I come in?"

China could not make a sound. What was *he* doing here? She thought she had made it perfectly clear that she never wanted to see him again. How dare he turn up here after what he had done?

"China?"

She looked up into Dereck's eyes, but she was so angry that she still couldn't find her voice. Also, she could feel Byron's gaze on her and knew he was watching to see what she would do. She realized then that she had moved into another world, a world that didn't include her ex-fiancé. In fact, incredibly, he seemed to be far, far in her past, and yet, he was here, standing before her.

She forced herself to remain calm. There was nothing to do but deal with the situation. He had come a long way, but this time she would make it clear that he shouldn't have bothered.

"Yes, of course. Come in." She opened the door wide, and she didn't miss the brief flare of surprise in his dark eyes when he saw Byron sitting on the couch.

"Dereck, this is Byron Scott. Byron, Dereck Morehouse, my ex-fiancé." Amazingly her voice sounded very impersonal.

Hearing the familiar name, Blue began to call out, "Oh, Dereck, it feels so good."

China didn't know whether to laugh hysterically or strangle the little bundle of feathers. Dereck had taught him to say that, finding it highly amusing when he said it in front of their friends. Now China saw that no one was laughing.

The two men measured each other warily, but Byron stood up and extended his hand first. Dereck didn't seem to know what to think. For a moment he stared at China awkwardly, as if expecting something more of an explanation. Clearly he wanted to know who this man was and why he was here, but China offered no further information. What on earth could she say? This is Byron, the man I just made love to in the shower?

"Sit down, Dereck," she said. "I'll get you something to drink."

"I'll do it," Byron said. He looked at the other man. "I can offer you a glass of white wine or coffee."

"Wine, please."

China watched as Byron nodded. She was pleased that he was sensitive to the situation, and she breathed a little easier when he had left the room.

"You must have had a difficult trip up here," she said as she joined Dereck on the couch. "I know the roads are washed out in some places."

"It was awful," he agreed, "and I had to walk part of the way to the cabin, but it was worth it. I had to see you."

China could feel the harsh beating of her heart; this was going to be very difficult. She wished Dereck hadn't come, but she was surprised that it didn't hurt to see him. Some part of her brain—she couldn't imagine which—was performing with amazing logic, and while she sat there, under incredible pressure, she began to make herself accept facts that she had known for a long time now but hadn't been able to face.

Dereck was no longer a part of her world; she had told him they were through, and they were. She realized at last that she was glad to have him out of her life, or at least he soon would be when he left. She meant to see to that. And she had Byron Scott to thank for that, too. If she hadn't met Byron, if she hadn't been distracted from her misery by him, made love to him—

Dereck interrupted her thoughts: "China, as I tried to tell you before, I've made an awful mistake," he began, but he fell silent again when Byron walked in with the wine. When Byron sat down in the chair, Dereck glanced at him resentfully, then took a long sip of his wine. China clasped her hands tightly together in her lap as she felt the tension building.

"Can I get you something to drink, China?" Byron asked, smiling warmly at her.

She shook her head. She couldn't swallow anything if her life depended upon it. All she wanted was to get this unpleasantness over with. She realized that Dereck had come a long way over bad roads to see her, but it was too late, much too late.

The minutes dragged by as they all sat there. China made an effort at light chatter, but she failed miserably.

Finally, Dereck spoke. "Why don't we go for a walk, China?"

She knew they needed to talk in private, but she wasn't looking forward to it. "Will you excuse us, please?" she asked, glancing at Byron.

"Yes, of course."

She turned to Dereck. "Let me put Blue up and get a jacket. I'll be right back." She saw that her hand was shaking as she walked back down the hall and put Blue in his cage. He was still calling "Oh, Dereck, it feels so good," and China was glad to shove him inside and shut him up.

"Who is that man and what's he doing here?" Dereck asked in a low, hard voice the minute he and China stepped outside.

She raised her shoulders in a careless gesture. "No one you know. He's a friend of Granny's."

"How long has he been in this cabin with you?"

"What do you want, Dereck?" she demanded, feeling much too uncomfortable with his questions. "It has something to do with our broken engagement or you wouldn't be here, so why don't we get it over with?" She was trying to remain composed, but it was terribly difficult. She still had some feeling for Dereck; she couldn't help it after all the time they had shared, all the plans they had made.

But somewhere along the way they had lost each other. Maybe their relationship had started to crumble as early as eight months before, when Dereck had canceled their wedding. China realized that for some time she had doubted that they would marry. She had seen the signs of Dereck's restlessness and not taken them for what they were. Now she saw all too clearly; she knew that the romance was really over.

Dereck gazed at her for a moment, then looked down at his hands as if he could somehow find the courage there to say what he wanted to say. He drew in a deep breath, then started walking toward the woods. China moved along beside him, feeling bad for them both.

Finally he cleared his throat and began to talk. "I was wrong, China. I love you. I want to marry you. None of the others mattered. It was only you I loved. Otherwise, I wouldn't have proposed. Please, give me another chance. Marry me. I swear I'll be true to you. I won't even look at another woman."

When he stopped and stared at her, the pleading look in his eyes almost weakened her resolve to be firm with him. She didn't want to hurt him; it didn't matter how deeply he had hurt her. She didn't think she could be cruel to him, but she knew she had to put him out of her life. It was all over between them; Byron had shown her that.

"I'm sorry, Dereck," she said in a thick voice that almost betrayed her, "but I'm going to Scotland with Byron."

She was as surprised as Dereck to hear herself say that; she hadn't known until just that moment that she had made up her mind. She had said it to make Dereck realize that there was no hope for them, but now she knew how much she really wanted to go. "I thought you understood that we were through. I thought that was what we both agreed on the last time we talked. If you'd called—"

"I tried to yesterday but I couldn't get through." China could see the color fade from Dereck's cheeks as he struggled to control his emotions. "China," he said hoarsely, "you can't be serious. You don't mean this. You're angry. You're hurt and I'm sorry for that. I know how betrayed you must feel, but I'll make it up to you. Give me the chance. The important thing is us— the two of us."

China shook her head. "Please don't make this any harder," she said softly. "It's over."

"And you're going to *Scotland*—with this—this *stranger?* I don't believe it! Who is he? Where did you meet him? Is he some man you picked up just to get even with me?"

"He is not!" China said, pride coming to her rescue. "I told you he is—*was* a friend of Granny's. He's an old friend of hers, and consequently of mine."

"That's no reason to leave the country with him. China, be reasonable. Don't do something you'll regret."

Oh, if only you knew, Dereck, that it's way too late for that, she wanted to say, but of course she didn't. "I'm sorry you drove all this way. I think it best that you leave now."

He startled her by grabbing her wrist. "Don't do this," he ordered. "Don't do this to us. We've spent three and a half years of our lives together. Don't throw it away because of your pride. We've been together too long."

China pulled free of his biting fingers. "That's just it, Dereck.

133

We *have* been together too long. Things have changed. I'm sorry."

Then she turned on her heel and walked back toward the house. Dereck caught up with her before she could open the door. Whirling her around, he demanded, "Did you leave me for that man?"

Stunned, China shook her head. "No, you left me, Dereck, a long time ago."

"I was wrong," he insisted. Unexpectedly he drew her to him, his embrace possessive and cruel. "You can't have forgotten me that easily," he groaned. "I won't let you." Then he tried to kiss her.

China turned her head and struggled to be free of his embrace, but he was too strong. They drew apart when Byron suddenly opened the door and stepped outside.

"I think you'd better let her go," he told Dereck in a voice like steel wrapped in velvet.

"What kind of game is this?" Dereck asked. "Do you know this is my fiancée? We were to have been married last week."

Byron nodded. "Sorry, fella. Your loss, my gain."

Rage was beginning to color Dereck's cheeks. "So you're content to take her off to Scotland, knowing that days ago she would have married me."

Byron looked a little surprised as he glanced at China, but he quickly recovered. "That's right. More than content—eager, in fact."

Before Dereck could behave rashly, China murmured, "Good-bye, Dereck. I'm sure it's all for the best."

For a brief moment she was afraid there was going to be trouble; then Dereck turned on his heel and walked away. China watched him briefly before she opened the door and went inside. She didn't want Byron to see how upset she was. She didn't love Dereck; she knew that now, but the knowledge hadn't come without some emotional cost. And Dereck had reminded her that she was asking for more of the same with Byron.

"You told him you were going with me?" Byron asked quietly when he had followed her into the room. He could see she was distressed, and he was afraid she had told Dereck they were going just to hurt him because she was hurting.

Wordlessly she nodded.

"Did you mean it?"

Tears were shimmering in her eyes when she looked at him. She straightened her back rigidly as if to give herself courage. "Of course I meant it. I'm sure we'll have a high old time there in merry Scotland."

Byron made himself smile. "Yes, I believe we will. I do believe we will." He studied her for a moment, trying to decide what to do next. "Can you get someone to toss your passport in the overnight mail?" he asked.

"Don't you know that I'm all packed already?" she asked bitterly. "Everything is right back there in the suitcase in my room—clothes, passport, deodorant, even motion-sickness pills."

"I see," Byron said, watching as China turned her back to him.

"I'm hungry," she said in a choked voice. "Why don't I go make some lunch for us?"

"Fine." He stared after her as she walked away, and wished there was something he could say to ease her pain, but he knew he couldn't help her now. She was too full of conflicting emotions—and he was part of them. Dereck really wasn't the man for her; Byron was sure of that. But then, he wasn't anybody's knight on a white horse either. So what now?

For a while he sat there brooding; then he got up and went to the telephone. Brooding never accomplished anything. He needed to act. The trip would be a good distraction for China, and he would love to see his grandparents. They were the salt of the earth, old-fashioned, and full of good common sense. They gave of themselves and asked nothing in return but decency and respect.

While China banged pots and pans around in the kitchen, more to release her pent-up feelings than anything else, Byron called a travel agent he knew in Monterey, and after very little time he had made the arrangements for the trip. He certainly wasn't as prepared as China to travel, but they would stay only a week. He could pick up some odds and ends in Monterey.

When China finally returned to the living room, Byron saw that she had made toasted cheese sandwiches for them. Canned Coke also sat on the tray, and Byron smiled a little. This wasn't his usual fare, but he was too hungry to object. It had been a hectic morning, and the breakfast of sweet rolls had hardly been substantial enough to last for long. He glanced at the clock and was surprised to see that it was already well into the afternoon. "Looks great," he said, taking the tray from China to set it on the coffee table. She nodded.

"Hey," he said, reaching out for her hand to draw her down on the couch, "do you want to talk about it?"

"About what?" she said, looking away from him.

Well, that answered his question, he told himself. *He* wanted to talk about it, but every time he tried to decide what he wanted to say, he was caught up in the same cycle. Was he going to pry into her life and try to find out how deep her love was for the man he had just seen? Was he going to tell her everything was going to be just fine? He wanted to make her that promise, but it wasn't within his power.

She picked up a Coke and took a sip of it.

"Are you a junk-food eater?" Byron asked lightly.

Unexpectedly, China laughed. "I am indeed, Mr. Restaurant Owner. I *love* junk food—hot dogs, hamburgers, and especially soft drinks."

Byron grinned, relieved to see that she was trying to get over her disappointment. "One day you'll be wearing it on your hips too," he teased.

"But not today," she retorted confidently. "Today I can boast thirty-six-inch hips that look approximately as they should."

"You can boast and I believe I can agree," Byron said, eyeing her appreciatively. He took the Coke from her hand and set it down. "In fact, let me check those hips, just to be sure."

She smiled, but she pushed his hands away, and Byron didn't know how far to go with her right now. He traced her sensuous lower lip with his thumb, and when her eyes met his, he saw the first glow of desire there. He lowered his head to kiss the full outline of her mouth, scattering quick kisses over it and drawing her lower lip in between his. When China responded by wrapping her arms around him, he saw that she needed the

136

physical contact. He drew her into his arms, holding her tightly to his chest as his mouth devoured hers.

China wanted desperately to be made love to again, to lose herself in the wonder and the ecstasy that Byron could create. She returned the fire she found in his kiss, and when he groaned hungrily with need, she felt a little thrill race over her skin. She wanted to stir his blood as he stirred hers, to please him as he did her. More than anything, right now she wanted to give herself up totally to the physical without all the anxiety that had plagued her all afternoon.

"Oh, China, how you excite me," Byron murmured against her ear, his breath warm and teasing. "You fit so perfectly to my body, as though you were made for me alone. I never knew how much I was missing before. I want to caress all of you, to feel all of you against me, thigh to thigh, hip to hip, chest to chest." His fingers fanned out over her breasts. "You have such lovely breasts," he whispered.

"You're not so bad yourself—for a blonde," she said with much more playfulness in her voice than she was feeling. "Is it true that blondes have more fun?"

Byron drew back from her for a moment to laugh huskily. "Well, by damn, let's find out," he said thickly. "Then *you* can tell *me.*" Suddenly he stood up, reached down, and easily lifted her in his arms, then started down the hall.

"I love carrying you," he said. "At first I was surprised that you didn't break my back, a big, long-legged thing like you."

His gray eyes were glittering with laughter, and China easily retorted, "And I was surprised you could lift anything—a fair-haired boy like you with a name like Junior."

"Come on, now, Che-Che," he said, "give me a break."

China closed her eyes and smiled, happy to give him as good as he gave her. More than anything, she just wanted to be in his arms.

Byron carried her to the bedroom, where he gently set her down on the bed. China watched him, waiting for him to join her, and when he did, she eagerly moved into his arms. His lips found hers again, and she let her tongue slip into the warmth of his mouth.

When Byron began to kiss her face and throat as he murmured sweet words to her, telling her how much he wanted her and how beautiful she was, China let herself drift into the rapture of his loving. He slipped her sweater and bra off, and when his warm mouth claimed the tip of one breast, she closed her eyes and let the erotic sensations absorb her conscious mind.

Byron was a tender but demanding lover. He made her want to give him all the pleasure he was giving her, and when he had removed the rest of her clothing, China undressed him. Her fingers were trembling, and she couldn't look into his face, but with the afternoon sunshine streaming in, she gazed admiringly at his beautiful golden body.

He stretched out beside her and she began to kiss him, letting her mouth trail down his blond-haired chest to his nipples. She ran her tongue around them as he had done to hers, and she felt Byron's fingers fan out through her long, dark tresses.

China moved down the length of Byron's body, letting her mouth and fingers tease and play lightly over his skin, biting and kissing the solid contours, exploring the sensitive areas, until she heard him hoarsely call her name.

"China, oh, China," he murmured passionately, reaching out to draw her back up into his arms. She stretched out on top of him, entwining her legs in his, feeling the hard length of him beneath her body. Then she began to move gently against him, arousing him further with her breasts and her hips while she kissed his mouth.

She was burning with need, and she knew the same fire was raging as hotly within him, but she wanted to prolong this delicious agony until they both could stand no more of the exquisite desire.

Byron's mouth was demandingly caressing hers, pouring oil on the wildfire running out of control inside her. His mouth left hers again and Byron eased her onto her back. His lips began to trace her curves, moving moistly down the crests and valleys of her body until China was the one to cry out in sweet torment.

"Byron! Byron!"

This time, when he rose to take her in his arms, he rolled over on his back again and drew her down on top of him. "Oh, Byron," China moaned as she felt him ease deep inside her, causing a river of thrills to radiate the length and breadth of her long, undulating body. He held her hips, controlling the pace of their passion, and China leaned forward, bending over his chest so that she could touch his mouth again with her own. His lips burned against hers, and his tongue thrust inside.

China couldn't get enough of this man. Her fingers spread out possessively over his chest and ran down the length of his body to where he joined so rapturously with her. Her touch spurred his passion and he felt the surging of his desire. She was driving him out of his mind, and he didn't think he could hold on to his sanity much longer.

At last he groaned thickly and brought her down hard on his body, losing himself in the beauty and the joy of her, sending part of him into her as they traveled together to the stars.

China's body trembled as it responded to Byron's passion as well as her own. Then, for a precious moment, she was lost somewhere in time and space, her eyes closed, relishing each wave of desire as it crashed over her body, carried her away, then receded.

When China finally opened her eyes to gaze down into Byron's, she saw that he was looking at her through glowing gray eyes, a satisfied smile on his face.

"*Do* blondes have more fun?" he asked thickly, his voice a husky growl, his hands gently stroking her skin.

"No," she said emphatically. "The raven-haired do. Oh, I swear to you they do." Her body was still throbbing with the aftermath of her passion and from the delights she had just savored.

Byron laughed a little. "Well, speak for yourself, woman. I'm sure I just had fun—a hell of a lot of it."

Giggling, China moved off his body to snuggle down by his side, and he drew her to him, molding her long length to his. "I'm glad," she whispered. "So did I."

She wouldn't let herself think beyond that statement or this moment. She wrapped her arms around Byron, and after a while she slipped into contented sleep.

139

CHAPTER TEN

China awakened to the warmth of Byron lying next to her. For a moment she wondered where she was, but when she opened her eyes and saw him, she smiled languorously.

Byron was propped up on one arm, watching her, and when he saw her smile he leaned forward to kiss her lips. *If this is heaven,* China thought to herself, *I'm willing to die.* She was drawn into his arms and relished the feel of his naked length pressed to hers.

The old bed gave as she moved, and China found herself wondering if Granny had known such bliss here in Grandpa's arms. *Grandpa's* arms, she reminded herself. Granny had been married when she made love in this bed. She had conceived her son here. She had slept here every night of her married life.

The thought dampened some of the joy she was feeling. Why couldn't she just take the here and now and live for this glorious moment? Why did she have to wonder what the future would bring? What would happen after they returned from their trip?

China drew away from Byron to pull the handmade quilt higher around her neck, and for the first time she realized that he had covered her while she was sleeping. She remembered falling asleep in his arms, on top of the covers.

"Where are you going, sexy woman?" Byron murmured.

China smiled at him. "Anywhere you are," she wanted to say. "Nowhere. I was just thinking about Scotland. If we are going, shouldn't we make some kind of arrangements?"

Byron grinned. "I already have. I know a travel agent in Monterey, and since I travel often, she creates miracles for me. We leave day after tomorrow. How's that for efficient?"

"Oh, I knew you would be *very* efficient," China teased. "I can tell you're a man who knows how to get things done."

"Here," he said, pulling her close again, "let me reinforce that idea for you."

China laughed lightly. She wanted more of his loving, but she had other things on her mind, too, other questions she needed to be reassured about.

"My, my, Che-Che," he murmured, "I think I'm going to love having you for a roommate."

Feeling herself withdrawing further, China forced a smile. A roommate. Was that all she was to be, then? A sleeping companion, should they happen to be in the house at the same time? The thought made her shiver, and Byron hugged her to his side.

"Surely you aren't cold," he said. "But if you are, I know just the way to warm you up."

Laughing lightly, China replied, "Yes, I'm sure you do." She met his steady gray eyes.

"Do you take all your roommates to Scotland?" she made herself ask.

"Only the ones I like best."

This conversation was making China feel worse and worse. Byron was keeping it all light and teasing, and it was clear that he wasn't going to indulge her insecurity about the casualness of their lovemaking. But he wasn't going to put her off anymore. There were things she needed to know.

"Who is Sara?" she asked, rightly expecting to erase the playful look from his face.

Byron regarded her coldly for a long moment before he replied. "My ex-wife."

"Oh, I see." And she was sure she did see. So he *had* been married, she thought in surprise. From the tense expression she saw on his face, there was no doubt in her mind that the experience hadn't been a good one.

"Is that why you can't make a commitment to any woman?" she asked boldly.

Now it was Byron's turn to withdraw. Damn, he told himself. He didn't want to talk about Sara. Why had he muttered her name in his delirium? He had stopped loving her so long ago, but by then she had already altered his life. He didn't want to think about China's question. It made him uncomfortable, and he dealt with it by putting her on the defensive.

"What are you trying to do?" he asked, attempting to keep his tone light and failing, "get a proposal out of me? I haven't proposed to a woman in many years, and it seems to work out best that way—for both of us."

China had no idea why his response should hurt so deeply. She did know how he felt about marriage. She shouldn't have been surprised by his reply.

She made herself shake her head. "Do you think I want to *marry* you just because we're sleeping together? You must have rocks in your head, Junior. I look for more than that in a lifetime mate. Anyway, I've had my fill of that marriage business." She tapped his chin lightly with her fist, amazed that her hand was steady enough to hit the target. "Right now you happen to be my roommate. Lucky you," she teased.

Byron laughed, and he wanted to draw her back into his arms, but he found that he could not. She had used his own words, but she had surprised him. Was he to be one in a line of men she would sleep with in this cabin? He had been sure she had had reservations about making love with him, but maybe he had been wrong. God knew, he had been wrong about women before in his time, but with China?

After all, he was just getting to know her, and unfortunately he was liking what he found very much until she told him how little their lovemaking had meant to her. Was she so bitter about Dereck that she was taking temporary refuge in his arms? Would any man's do? Hell, he didn't like the sound of this.

"Now, come on, Che-Che," he said, "if I asked you to marry me right now, what would you do?"

"Smile pleasantly and refuse," she replied quickly. She wasn't foolish enough to let him think that she would consider a marriage proposal from him, even if he was serious. Which he wasn't, and she knew it. Still, the mere thought of spending her lifetime with this man caused her heart to beat rapidly. Talk about waking up to heaven every day . . .

This time Byron was the one to laugh, but it was a forced laugh. "Smart girl," he told her. But her reply troubled him. And why shouldn't it? He was feeling more uncomfortable by the moment, and for the first time in his life he wanted to run away from a woman. Colleen's little granddaughter was turning him inside out, messing up his orderly life. He didn't like that.

"I don't know about you," he said, needing desperately to change the subject, "but I'm starving. We never did eat those sandwiches you made."

China smiled. "I'm sorry, Mr. Restaurant Man, but it's a little late for those." She moved out from under the covers, and when she saw Byron's eyes darken with instant desire, she grabbed the handiest piece of clothing, which happened to be his shirt. She slipped it over her head, not realizing that it was almost more provocative than her nude body.

The shirt barely reached her thighs and clung to her breasts, causing the nipples to appear pert and inviting. Her long, slender legs seemed to go on forever, shapely and enticing, and Byron couldn't stop looking at her.

"I'll make fresh sandwiches," she offered. Then she turned her back to him and left the room. She needed to keep busy. She wanted to forget about what he had said. She wanted to believe that she was important to him. The last thing she wanted was to be merely another woman to him. No, unfortunately she wanted much more.

She told herself that she should cancel the trip to Scotland and go back home, but she didn't want to do that either. She was going to see this thing through to the end. If nothing else, it would be a valuable lesson for her. Besides, she wanted her allotted time with Byron Scott. He was still the most exciting man she had ever known.

China had already put the sandwiches on to cook when the phone rang. There was only one in the house, and she went to the living room to answer it. It was Karly, telling her that dinner would be ready in an hour. Darn it, she had forgotten all about Karly's dinner invitation.

"Oh, Karly, I don't want you to go to that trouble," China said.

"What trouble?" was Karly's response. "I put a roast and vegetables in the crock pot. In a bit I'll brown the meat. That's all there is to it, and we're so looking forward to seeing you and Byron. We had such a nice visit last night."

"Yes, we did too" China agreed. "Fine. We'll be over in an hour." She could smell the cheese sandwiches start to burn and wanted to get off the phone.

"Come early," Karly coaxed. "Randolph will fix us hot toddies before dinner."

"Great. See you soon," China said. Then she quickly hung up the phone.

By the time she got back to the kitchen, the sandwiches were black on one side. "Oh, darn it," she groaned. Then she smiled to herself and deliberately turned them over. She turned the heat off, but the pan was so hot that the fresh side of the sandwich quickly turned black, the cheese running out of it all around.

China carefully put the sandwiches on plates and placed them on a tray. Then she got two more Cokes out of the refrigerator. "I'll do something for you, Junior," she muttered, "that your other women wouldn't dream of doing." Smiling blissfully to herself, she walked back down the hall to Granny's room.

"Did I smell something burning?" Byron asked, sniffing the air suspiciously.

"Just a little," China said with a smile. "Karly called, and the sandwiches got a little overdone."

Byron looked at the blackened bread distastefully. "A little?" he echoed. He hated to see what she called a lot, but he didn't want to hurt her feelings, and when she offered him a plate, he took it.

He stared at the sandwich, wondering if she really expected him to eat it. How he wished he had taken time to eat the last one before he had made love to China. At least that one had appeared to be properly cooked. He made himself smile at her, then picked up the sandwich and bit into it.

Watching him with barely contained laughter, China picked up her sandwich as if she were going to follow suit. Byron swallowed the bite he had in his mouth and quickly washed it down with Coke.

"Is it all right?" China asked eagerly.

"To tell you the truth—"

"I hope it's okay," China interrupted him. "We don't have any more cheese."

144

Thank God for small favors, Byron told himself. He tried to take another bite, but the thing was just two black boards with melted cheese coating the ends. "China, I'm not as hungry as I thought," he said at last. He wasn't going to eat the damned thing. He wasn't hungry now, after tasting it.

Suddenly, China put her own sandwich down and burst into laughter. "I sure as heck wouldn't eat it," she said, watching him between bouts of laughter.

He looked puzzled for a moment; then he set his plate on the table, reached out for China, and dragged her onto the bed. "You little witch," he growled. "I didn't want to hurt your feelings. That's why I took a bite. You're going to pay for that."

China was still laughing as Byron lifted up the shirt hem and began to nibble on her thighs. "Byron, no," she cried. "Don't bite me!"

But he was relentless, and he began to move farther up her legs. "No," she cried again, trying to sit up as she remembered Karly's call. "We've got to get dressed and go over to the Davises."

"The hell we do," he said, his words muffled against her flesh.

China tugged on his blond curls. "I'm serious," she said earnestly. If he kept on, she wouldn't even be able to recall that she'd promised Karly they'd be over. "Karly asked us to dinner last night and she's got it almost ready. They want us to come over now for hot toddies."

"And you agreed?" Byron said, looking up at her with incredulous eyes.

She nodded, then broke into laughter again. "I didn't know you had other plans."

At last Byron grinned at her. "You're an evil witch," he announced, pulling the shirt back down. "I don't think I could survive being your roommate all the time."

"You couldn't," she said, but her voice had lost its humor. "You couldn't handle a woman like me." When he grabbed for her again, she skillfully evaded his hands and jumped off the bed.

Byron watched her for a moment with passion-darkened eyes. He had a feeling that he would like to give it a try, handling a woman like her. Then he brushed the thought away. He had to get dressed. The last thing he wanted to do that night was visit with Karly and Randolph, but he couldn't disappoint them so late.

China had already left the room, and Byron could hear her next door, talking to Blue. He remembered that damned parrot saying "Oh, Dereck, it feels so good," and he felt like going in and cramming his fist down its gizzard. He found himself wondering how he measured up to Dereck, and he laughed at the ridiculousness of the thought. He could care less—or could he?

"Damn you, Colleen," he muttered aloud.

He was still grumbling to himself, something he had never done until he met China, when he heard her go into the bathroom and turn on the shower. As he found his robe and pulled it on he resisted the urge to join her. Instead he went to her room to make sure that the bird had been put safely away. Then he went to the library and let Demon out.

The black cat stretched languidly, happy to see him. Byron glanced at the cat's litter box and the toy mouse lying on the floor on its side. Not exactly all the comforts of home, he told himself as he reached down and picked Demon up. "How are you doing, fella? I hope it's not too hard on you, being shut up in here, but what choice have I?"

The cat purred contentedly, and Byron took him to the kitchen and gave him a treat. As he watched the cat eat he reminded himself that the animal was only four years old. With luck he would live ten or more years. He had heard that parrots lived thirty or forty years. He wasn't getting rid of his animal, and he was sure China wouldn't get rid of the parrot. How long could they keep juggling the animals like this, keeping one here and the other there?

"You do have rocks in your head," he muttered aloud when the implication of what he was thinking hit him. He would take his cat and go home. China would take her bird and go home. That would solve that problem. Marriage wasn't for him; he had discovered that long ago.

He spun around when China walked into the kitchen. "Oh, the black devil is running loose," she said. "I wanted to let Blue get a little exercise before we went to the Davises."

146

"That's all Demon's doing—getting a little exercise and a little attention," Byron said, smiling at her. Her skin was rosy from her shower, and the ends of her dark hair were damp. She was dressed in her jeans again, and a pale blue sweater. She smelled of sweet soap and faint perfume, and Byron hoped she had put the lilac scent on just for him.

"I'll take him back to the library when he's through eating."

"I feel guilty about having to keep him in there," China admitted.

"Why, China, I didn't know you cared," he teased.

"I care about all animals. It's something Granny taught me. She loved the wildlife around here, and she always told me that each and every thing under God's heaven had the right to be there."

Byron smiled at her. He liked this girl Granny Castleberry had influenced in so many ways. She was sensitive and good-natured and caring. She wore her sexy nightgowns for him, but she didn't mind him seeing her without makeup. She had split his head with a vase, but she had also stayed up all night caring for him. She had served him a burned sandwich, but she worried about his cat.

"Oh, Byron, you're losing it, ol' boy," he muttered aloud.

China looked at him curiously, amused to hear him talking to himself. "What did you say?"

Surprised that he had muttered aloud when she could hear him, Byron gazed thoughtfully at her. "I said that ever since you bashed me with that pitcher of flowers, I've had rocks in my head. Or are they pieces of pottery?"

"As hard as your head is, mister, they have to be rocks," she retorted, smiling.

Byron returned her smile, his eyes gleaming. Then he moved toward her purposefully. China stood her ground. "Stay back, you sex maniac!" she said, her eyes glowing with merriment.

"I'll show you what a sex maniac really is," Byron said in a low, husky voice. He grabbed her before she could protest again and pulled her to him. His mouth trapped hers, his tongue dipping inside to sample the honeyed treasure to be found there. He molded his body tightly to hers, making her aware of his potent masculinity.

147

China wrapped her arms around his neck. She couldn't seem to help herself. He stirred her senses in a way she had never thought possible. He was kissing her wickedly, playfully, making growling noises in his throat as he held her in his arms, dipping her toward the floor. Then he scattered hot, moist kisses down her throat. When he finally released her, she was breathing raggedly.

She smiled, but she was alarmed by the way his kisses aroused her. She actually wanted to go back to bed with him. She couldn't seem to think of anything else but making love as long as Byron was around. Nevertheless she made herself say, "You should get dressed. I told Karly we'd be over soon."

"I know it, damn you," he joked. "I have better things to do than visit."

China shook her head. "Oh, no you don't. I promised."

"Well, far be it from me to cause a lady to break her promise," he said, bending down to pick up Demon.

China fought against the urge to run her fingers through his curls. She had almost reached out when he stood up, causing her to stifle the impulse.

"The house is all yours. Let that dirty-mouthed parrot roam free."

For a moment China was taken aback by his comment; then she remembered the last thing that Blue had said. She smiled to herself. So his crack about Dereck hadn't been lost on Byron. Good. She was glad he had said it. With light steps, she went into her room and opened the cage.

Blue was back to his favorite phrase. "Thanks a lot," he sang out.

"You're entirely welcome," she murmured sweetly. "And thank you, you clever little bundle of feathers." She lowered her voice and said, "Say 'Oh, Dereck, it feels so good.'"

But this time Blue wasn't in the mood. "Here I am. Where's the party?" he crowed energetically.

"You're a ham," she told him. Then she took him to the living room and sat down with him. Blue soon flew over to his standing perch and sat on it, squawking boisterously, saying nothing intelligible.

A short time later Byron joined them. He was dressed in

148

navy slacks and a V-neck pullover sweater in a deep gold color that set off his own golden handsomeness. China's gaze roamed over him appreciatively, and she told herself that it was no wonder he had so many women after him.

The thought bothered her. Dereck had already become only a shadow in her mind, a memory less exciting than the mere thought of Byron Scott. She recalled her grandmother saying that all things work out for the best, but what would that mean in this situation? That Byron would help her get through this readjustment period, then vanish from her life? And who then would help her get over Byron?

"Why don't you put that bunch of feathers up so we can go," Byron suggested.

China nodded, and when she walked over to Blue, he sang out, "Oh, Dereck, do it again."

"Not now, dummy," China muttered under her breath. "You already had your chance with that one."

"Not now dummy," Blue muttered in a low buzzing tone.

Glancing at Byron to see if he had heard, China hurried down the hall with the parrot on her finger. "I can't say anything to you," she chastised the bird.

"Not now, dummy," he said again.

"Dummy is right," China agreed. "Dummy should never have said that."

"Not now, dummy," Blue said again. And just to make sure China understood him, he repeated it three times, imitating the tone in which she had spoken.

As though in reconciliation, he said "Kiss, kiss" as she started to put him in the cage.

"Oh, all right." China kissed him on his beak, and he cooed contentedly as she put him in the cage and covered it.

Byron was smiling to himself when China returned to the living room. "What do you find so amusing?" she asked.

He shook his head. "I'll be damned if I know. Every time I see you with that silly little parrot, I want to grab you up in my arms and smother you with kisses." He seemed thoughtful for a moment, then crossed the room to her. "In fact," he murmured, "why just talk about it?"

When he reached for her, China stepped back. "Oh, no," she

said. "We have an evening engagement and I mean to keep it. Come on, lover boy, Karly and Randolph are waiting."

Byron nodded. "So they are."

Linking his arm with hers, he guided her toward the back door. It was already dusk, and China shivered as they walked through the trees leading to the small cabin.

Byron wrapped his arm around her shoulder. "You should have worn a jacket."

"I thought the sweater would be enough," she replied.

He tightened his grip. "I'll keep you warm."

China laughed lightly. She had no doubt about that. In fact, he kept her so warm that she could hardly think of anything but him when he was near. She was acutely aware of him as they made their way to the cabin.

Once they were inside, Karly led them back to the kitchen, which was filled with the wonderful aroma of pot roast. Randolph was in his rocking chair, smoking his pipe, and China saw that Karly had put some other comfortable chairs near the roaring fire.

Soon they were all gathered around the fireplace, chatting happily and drinking the hot toddies Randolph had prepared. But even as China enjoyed the warmth and closeness of Byron and her friends, she couldn't keep from thinking about the future. Would these times with Byron be all she would ever have? Would he take her to Scotland, then slip out of her life forever?

Not forever, she reminded herself. He still owned half her house. But would that be her only tie to him? She didn't think she could stand it if it were.

CHAPTER ELEVEN

Karly hadn't yet set the table, and China was glad to have something to do when she offered to help and the other woman unexpectedly agreed. But as they approached the table China found that her friend had an ulterior purpose.

"Maybe Colleen's going to have her way after all," the older woman said in a soft, low voice.

"What do you mean?" China asked, but she knew all too well what Karly was talking about.

"Why, you and Junior, of course. Honey, I can tell he's in love by the way he looks at you. It's just a real shame the two of you didn't meet sooner, when Colleen was alive. She would have loved to see this. It was her fondest wish."

China wanted to tell Karly that Byron wasn't in love—he was in lust—but she wouldn't do that, of course. And she could only thank God that Granny *wasn't* alive to see her and Byron. She knew the old woman never would have approved of the way they were carrying on.

"Karly . . ." China began, but what was there to say?

Her friend looked at her expectantly, and China lowered her gaze, staring at the plates as she took them out of the cupboard. "Byron isn't in love with me."

"You can't fool an old romantic like me," Karly said, whispering. "I see all the right signs. First thing you know, that boy'll be proposing marriage." She glanced at China without bothering to hide the pleased glow in her green eyes. "And, China, when Junior makes marriage plans, he won't be doing any backing out at the last minute. You can take my word for that."

"He doesn't want to get married," China replied quietly. She

151

could hear Byron talking animatedly with Randolph and wasn't worried about being overheard, but how she wished she wasn't involved in this conversation at all.

Karly patted China's shoulder. "We'll just see about that."

China wanted to laugh bitterly, but instead she made herself smile and walk over to the table with the plates.

When they had set the table, Karly called Byron and Randolph. As China watched the young man walk beside the old one, she wondered who would be there with Byron when he was Randolph's age. And she was swiftly reminded that she did indeed want a companion for all the years of her life.

She didn't care what other women said about all that being passé, about women needing to take charge of their own destinies and live their own lives. She was a contemporary woman in all the ways that counted: She worked, she supported herself, she mingled well socially, and she could survive on her own without a man. But why miss out on all the love and wonder that was to be had by sharing life with one person?

Byron could flit from woman to woman all his life. He could gather a list of lovers so long that he couldn't remember their names. But was that for her? China didn't think so. She wanted what Karly and Randolph had. She wanted what Granny and Grandpa had had. She wanted what her own mother and father had.

She knew marriage wasn't the perfect state, but what was? She knew about conflict and discontent, but that was part of life. She had that right now.

She knew, too, that a piece of paper didn't make a couple happy. The two people involved had to do that. She knew dozens of couples who lived together and seemed perfectly happy, but at least they, too, had some kind of commitment. They were sharing their lives, presumably on a long-term basis.

Shaking her head, China tried to free it of the troublesome thoughts. She had gone to bed with Byron knowing full well what she was doing. And she had loved every moment of it. She wasn't going to keep punishing herself for it. And she wasn't going to let Karly's overly romantic view of the situation keep her from enjoying whatever time she had left with Byron.

Byron pulled out a chair for her, and when she had sat down

next to him, she gave her attention to the meal. The meat was so tender that it fell apart on the platter when Karly began to serve it. China realized she was absolutely famished, and when her plate was filled with meat and vegetables, she began to eat, concentrating on the delicious food.

Karly and Randolph were doing most of the talking, while Byron and China ate as if it were their last meal. Finally, Karly broke into laughter. "Aren't you two eating anything over there?" she asked. "You both act as if you're starving."

Byron and China looked at each other in embarrassment, then laughed. "I fixed cheese sandwiches a couple of times today, but both times they were inedible," China offered. She didn't bother to tell them why.

"Well, I declare, honey," Karly said, "all you have to do is put mayonnaise and cheese on bread. Good heavens, Junior," she said, turning to him, "you should know that too."

Byron and China laughed again. "Karly, honestly, we both know how to make a cheese sandwich. It's just that—that I toasted them and let them burn."

"Well," the older woman mused, "you sure seem to be taking good care of Junior. First you hit him over the head and then you try to starve him." Everyone laughed at that, including China.

"Say, Junior, some of the boards are down on the back fence bordering the Naples property," Randolph said, changing the subject adeptly. "I'm getting some wood next week, and I was wondering if you could help me work on the fence?"

"Any other time you know I'd be happy to," Byron said, glancing at China, "but I won't be here next week."

"Why, you aren't going back to Santa Monica already, are you?" Karly asked. "I thought you said you were going to be here for two weeks."

China carefully kept her eyes on her plate while Byron answered: "I'm going to Scotland."

China knew what was coming, and she braced herself for it. "Well, I declare. I thought you and China were enjoying getting to know each other." China could feel Karly's green gaze on her face. "That'll leave you all alone over there, China. Now, I want you to come over here and have meals with Randolph and me. Apparently you aren't bothering to eat right on your own."

Looking up, China met the other woman's eyes. She forced a smile. "Thank you, Karly, but I'm going with Byron."

The old woman blinked. For a moment she was taken aback by the news. Then she smiled. "Well, how wonderful for you." She nodded at Byron. "I know the two of you will have a lovely time." But China saw disapproval in her glance. This obviously wasn't what Karly had had in mind when she envisioned the couple falling in love.

"My grandparents live in Scotland. We'll be staying with them," Byron said.

That seemed to make everything all right again. "That's real nice," Karly said. "I remember you telling me you had grandparents in some foreign country."

Byron nodded. "Being here on Colleen's land with her granddaughter has made me miss my own grandparents. They're getting on in years, and I want to spend a little time with them."

"How nice for them *and* you," Karly said.

The meal was resumed with the same degree of pleasantness for everyone but China. Karly might have been reassured by the fact that the couple would be chaperoned by Byron's grandparents, but China knew that the only threat Byron offered was to her heart, and that threat would not simply disappear as long as he was at her side. And maybe even longer than that.

Despite the fact that the flight to Scotland had taken many hours and China was exhausted from jet lag and the time change, when the plane landed in Edinburgh, she was even more thrilled than she had expected to be. This was a dream come true for her, and she was as excited as a child.

She was filled with carefree exuberance. Blue had been left in Karly's care, and Demon had been left at Byron's father's house. All China wanted to concentrate on was Scotland—and, of course, Byron.

It was late afternoon; he had rented a car to take them to his grandparents' house, and although China knew how excited he must be about seeing them, she asked, "Can we just drive through the city on the way, so I can have a peek at it before we go to the house?"

He smiled at her, clearly enjoying her enthusiasm. "How tired are you?"

She shook her head. "Not very. I managed to sleep some on the plane."

Nodding, he replied, "Yes, I did notice that. You used my shoulder for a pillow."

"Oh, I hope you didn't mind."

"No," he said with a grin, "In fact, I rather enjoyed it." He winked at her. "And since you're such a delight, I'll tell you what we'll do: We'll see the castle and just a few brief highlights of the city before we leave it."

China knew that Byron had called another relative to be sure that the old folks hadn't planned to be out of the area, although he had said there was little chance of that, since they stayed close to home. They wouldn't be expecting visitors, and while China thrilled to the prospect of seeing the castle, she shook her head. "Oh, I can't ask you to do that. I know how badly you want to see your grandparents. Just a quick ride through town will hold me until we can come back."

"You just think it will," he said. "Seeing the sights in Edinburgh is like eating potato chips: One is never enough."

China laughed. "I won't argue with you. I'd love to see the castle."

"We've barely arrived in time," Byron explained. "The season is just about over, and some of the attractions close during the winter, but don't worry, there's plenty to see."

"I know," China said. "Dereck and I had booked one of the last tours available from our agent. She said she didn't advise going after the end of October because of the weather."

She hadn't meant to mention Dereck's name again in front of Byron, but it had come out so naturally. She and Dereck had pored over the brochures of England, Ireland, Scotland, and Wales, spending hours deciding which tour they wanted to take.

"I see," Byron said, but it was plain to China that her comment had taken some of the fun out of the trip for him, and she vowed that she would do her best to keep quiet and let Byron show her the country the way he wanted to.

155

He drove directly to the castle, and for a little while China was lost in her thoughts. Then Byron said, "There, look up on that hill."

Her first glimpse of Edinburgh Castle took her breath away. There it stood in all its magnificence, more splendid than any picture could ever portray it, its magic and mystery even more pronounced than she had expected it to be. High above the city, standing on an extinct volcano, the castle dominated the skyline, etching itself against the stark sky.

"Oh, Byron!" she cried, "It's even more wonderful than I had anticipated."

"It *is* incredible," he agreed. "It was built up on the hill deliberately to make it an impregnable fortress. The stone edifices there on Castle Rock were regularly under siege for nearly five hundred years, but the castle was never successfully stormed. Nevertheless it has been captured and recaptured many times over the centuries. That old castle has served as a fort, palace, prison, arsenal, armory, and garrison."

As Byron drove up to the castle he began to tell China a little about Scotland's turbulent history, including the fact that the name *Scotland* actually came from a Gaelic-speaking tribe from Ireland called Scots. China listened attentively, eager to absorb all she could about this place, which fascinated her so.

When they had parked the car and were walking toward the two Royal Scots guards posted at the first gate leading up the cobblestone ramp to the castle, Byron said, "No one is sure exactly when Edinburgh's history began, but a stone fortification was erected in the seventh century and the first actual castle was built in the eleventh century."

China glanced up at the black naval cannon jutting through the ramparts, and Byron smiled. "Those have never been fired, but we'll see the cannon that booms out over the city each weekday at one P.M."

"Most cities mark time at noon," China commented. "Why does Edinburgh do it at one?"

Byron laughed. "This is Scotland. Why waste twelve cannon shots when you can use one?"

China laughed with him. She had heard all those terms that were usually applied to the Scots: *frugal, dour, hard-drinking, humorless.* Now she could see for herself if they had any validity.

The tour of the castle was fascinating, from the Esplanade to the Scottish United Services Museum, and China especially enjoyed seeing tiny St. Margaret's Chapel, the last building they visited.

"It was the Saxon Queen Margaret who is given credit for playing a large part in the development of Edinburgh in the eleventh century," Byron explained. "Wife of Malcolm III, who incidentally was son of Shakespeare's Duncan and successor to Macbeth, Margaret convinced Malcolm that this civilized area was best for a home, and the crude rock fortress was converted into royal living quarters."

"I want to buy some books and read up on all of this," China exclaimed.

"They do have a gift shop here," Byron said, "but we can go to a bookstore and get everything you want tomorrow. It's getting late."

"Fine," China agreed, letting Byron take her hand to lead her out of the chapel. He guided her to the stone wall so that they could admire the spectacular view from their lofty vantage point.

As China gazed over the city spread out below them, its lights glittering and twinkling in the twilight, creating a magic, fairy-tale beauty, she murmured, "It's wonderful, Byron, simply wonderful."

"This is the real Scotland," he told her in a low voice. "I wanted you to see it."

When she looked into his glowing gray eyes, she could tell that he was enjoying her pleasure almost as much as she. "Thank you for bringing me," she said softly.

"I wouldn't have missed it." His eyes held hers, and she was unable to look away despite the magnificent view beyond him. Suddenly he lowered his head and kissed her, his lips burning enticingly against hers.

China wrapped her arms around his neck, his touch causing her to forget momentarily all the splendor around her. She felt as if they were the only two people here, caught up in a world of their own, and for a moment she was lost in the wonder of it.

157

Byron was the one to draw away. "We'd better be on our way before I forget all about my grandparents," he said thickly.

China gave him an understanding smile, and she was feeling breathless as, hand in hand, they took the steep, winding flight of steps known as Lang Stairs down to the bottom of the castle.

When they reached the car, Byron said, "Perhaps later tonight we'll come back for a little nightlife if you're up to it."

"I'd like that," China said warmly. As they drove through the city she stared out the window at the passing scenery, fascinated by all the sights around her, eager to get out and explore more of Edinburgh.

She was enchanted by fast-paced Princes Street, with its West Princes Street Gardens, Edinburgh's comely green centerpiece, and she fell in love with the neoclassical New Town's stately Georgian architecture. She marveled at Charlotte Square, which Byron told her was considered the most noble square in Europe.

She hoped that they could come back that night after they had spent some time with Byron's grandparents, and she was pleased that he had mentioned it. He seemed to understand her enthusiasm so well.

The city gave way to more beautiful hill country, and China gazed in delight at the cottages and farms along the roadside. She could even see sheep roaming about. So the rural, wild Scotland *did* still exist. It reminded her of Big Sur, and she smiled secretly to herself.

"My grandparents live about half an hour from town," Byron explained. "They have a small farm that's been in the family for who knows how many years. It's in the valley, in the midst of some of the most gorgeous country in Scotland." He pointed out at the countryside. "Those bushes are gorse, and that's heather over there."

Eventually they took the back roads to a pretty little two-story cottage set back against a hill in the midst of pine woods. Byron had turned the car lights on, and when they flashed across the front of the house as he drove up to it the porch light came on and a stout, elderly woman poked her head out the door.

158

"That's my grandmother," he said, his voice animated. "She'll be so surprised to see us."

The old woman frowned as Byron shut off the car engine. Clearly she didn't recognize the vehicle, and she was wondering who had come calling.

But the instant Byron stepped out of the car, she called out excitedly to her husband. "Duncan. Duncan. We have visitors!"

China could hardly make out the words; the woman was speaking English, but not English as China knew it, and the thick Scots accent was difficult for her to understand.

Byron walked around to open China's door, and taking her by the arm, he led her up to the house. "Grandmother, it's me, Byron."

The woman's eyes widened in astonishment; then suddenly she rushed forward, murmuring some Scottish endearment China couldn't make out. She wrapped her arms around her grandson and tears began to stream down her face. The reunion was so moving that China had to look away, her own eyes filling with tears.

Soon an old man hurried out and joined in the hugging. Finally, Byron turned to include China.

"Grandmother, Grandfather, this is China Castleberry. She's the granddaughter of Gene and Colleen Castleberry. I'm sure you've heard father speak of them. Gene was a friend of father's for years."

"Yes, yes," the woman said. "You're so welcome to our house. Come in. Come in. It's brisk out."

She rolled her *r*'s, and China found the accent delightful, but she had to pay careful attention to the words. She extended her hand and offered the couple a smile. "Thank you."

They ushered Byron and China inside, and both old people began to talk at once about how Byron should have let them know he was coming so they could have prepared for him and his guest.

But China saw that they need not have worried. The house was spotless, the furniture sturdy but well used. A fire was roaring in the mammoth fireplace to drive back the chill wind and damp mist that hung over the Scottish countryside.

"We wanted to surprise you," Byron told them. "Now, don't

159

go to a lot of trouble. We'll be spending most of our time eating out and sight-seeing. China has never been to Scotland before."

Grandfather Scott turned to stare at his guest. "You'll love it here, lassie," he assured her. "Scotland soon steals the heart of every tourist who comes to visit." His old blue eyes twinkled merrily, and his mouth was wreathed in a smile beneath his shaggy mustache.

"China," Byron said, "my grandparents, Duncan and Hilliary Scott."

"This is such a pleasure," China said. "I hope we won't be an imposition."

Hilliary wrapped her arms around her grandson again. "Of course not. We're absolutely delighted." She looked at China. "Thank you, both. It warms an old woman's heart."

She freed her grandson. "Duncan help them bring in the luggage." Then she frowned thoughtfully. "Give Byron his father's old room, and for China the room which once belonged to Anne." She turned away. "I'll bring something to eat. You must be starving."

"Don't start fussing about," Byron insisted, but the old woman had made up her mind.

"I'll get tea and cakes for you, then start dinner. For you we shall have a typical Scottish meal," she told China, her eyes glowing in anticipation.

"Oh, please don't go to any bother," China said.

"It's no bother. We all must eat, and I have haggis left from yesterday."

China had heard of haggis, and she wasn't in any hurry to try it. By all accounts it was something non-Scots were wary of. She couldn't quite remember what it was, and she wasn't entirely sure she wanted to find out.

"May I help?" she asked politely.

Hilliary shook her head. "Oh, no. You're our guest."

China went out to the car with the men, but they wouldn't let her do anything, so for a few minutes she simply stood and inhaled the brisk Scottish air. It was downright cold, she decided, and she soon returned to the house despite her appreciation of the tranquil scene.

She followed Byron and Duncan upstairs, where they left her

luggage in a pretty room decorated with feminine frills. Then the two men eagerly took China on a tour of the house. Duncan pointed out the water closet, which Byron renamed the bathroom, and they all laughed.

In minutes she returned to her room and began to unpack. Byron's room was down the hall, and he stopped by to ask if everything was all right.

"Byron," she said, taking his arm and whispering quietly, "Hilliary says she's going to have haggis. I've heard it's awful."

He laughed. "No, honestly, it's not. That's a rumor started by foreigners. You must try it. I think you'll like it."

"What is it?"

"It's made from the sheep's finely chopped heart, liver, and lung. That's boiled with onions, beef suet, oatmeal, and seasoning inside a sewn-up sheep's paunch. It's served with bashed neeps and tatties."

"What the heck is that?" China muttered. "A disease?"

"Turnips and mashed potatoes," Byron said, laughing delightedly.

"Oh, thank heavens. Can't I just eat the vegetables? That haggis sounds a little—odd," she murmured in an attempt to be tactful.

"Come on, woman. You've got more sporting blood than that, I know. Try it, at least."

"Oh, Byron," she moaned, "have mercy."

"Nonsense," he said, dismissing her objections. "I'm going to unpack." He made a face. "I'm way down at the end of the hall. I told you these people are the salt of the earth. Did I also tell you they're old-fashioned?"

"Meaning they don't want you sleeping with your women here?" she asked flippantly, amazed at how the thought of him being here with another woman hurt.

He smiled but he said sincerely, "I've never brought another woman here."

"Oh, lucky me," she quipped. But as she watched him walk away, she did feel lucky. And in spite of herself she could not help but wonder if that meant Byron considered her special.

It was only a matter of minutes before Hilliary called them downstairs. She served the tea and cakes in the living room.

"Now, you three sit down," she said, including Duncan, "and eat this while I get dinner ready." Then she bustled away.

"It won't do any good to protest," Duncan said, grinning as he seated himself and poured a cup of tea. "Sit down. Eat."

Byron winked at China. "You'll like the cakes," he said, settling in a comfortable wing chair. "They're oatcakes." He picked up a dish and began to put some of its contents on the oatcake. "This is *crowdie*, Scotland's ancient version of cottage cheese. Here, try it."

China joined him, and when she sampled the oatcake with crowdie, she found that she liked it very much. "It's quite good," she said.

Duncan gave her a pleased smile. "You're going to love Scotland, lassie," he predicted.

"I already do," she said. "It's just beautiful."

The three of them began to talk about the sights Byron and China had already seen and what they intended to see the next day, and it wasn't long before Hilliary summoned them to the kitchen. She had set the table with her best china, and she was smiling proudly when she indicated which chair each of them should take.

China regarded the haggis without enthusiasm, but when she bravely tried it, she found that it really was rather tasty. Byron winked at her as she complimented Hilliary, and he seemed pleased that she had been gracious enough to sample the dish Hilliary had so happily served.

Soon the four of them were chatting pleasantly. The grandparents wanted to hear all the news from the States, each and every detail about Byron senior, and Byron patiently answered all their questions. China was moved by the love she sensed between them. She had had a special relationship like that with Granny, and she found herself thinking that Byron was lucky to have his father's parents both still alive.

The only awkward moment came when Hilliary unexpectedly asked, "So, then, Byron, have you brought this young lady here to introduce her to us as your future bride?" Her eyes were dancing, and clearly she was excited by the prospect.

"Now, hold on," Byron said swiftly. "Don't start planning weddings. China is only a friend."

Byron picked up his fork and began to eat again, but he was cursing himself for having answered so defensively, so quickly. China was more than a friend and they both knew it. Of course his grandmother had thought the woman with her grandson was something special. He hadn't even brought Sara here, but then, Sara had been to Scotland several times, and she hadn't been especially interested in making a trip just to meet his grandparents.

Hell, he thought unhappily to himself, he didn't know what he was doing here with China. He didn't think anything or anyone was going to lure him into marriage again, but China had his emotions all twisted around. He wasn't sure himself what bringing her here meant to him; he only knew he wanted to forget the disappointed expression on his grandmother's face. And for some reason he could not even look at China.

Lowering her gaze, China bit back rising bitterness. It took her a moment to swallow the lump in her throat, and when she finally forced herself to look up at Hilliary, she, too, was aware of the disappointment and also the questions written in those clear brown eyes.

China smiled faintly and toyed with the idea of saying that she and Byron had both inherited her Granny's house, but it would have been too complex to explain.

When she looked at Byron, she saw that he was eating as though nothing out of the ordinary had been said, and she followed his example, but it was difficult. She could not help remembering that moment they had shared at the castle. She had felt a spark of something strong and glowing then, she was certain, but somehow that spark had gone out.

Now she wished that she hadn't come at all. She would be embarrassed to have the old folks know how intimate her relationship with Byron was. Then she realized that here in his grandparents' house she wouldn't be sleeping with him. She didn't know whether to laugh or cry, for she knew that she wanted to spend her nights in his arms—what few nights she had left with him.

The pain the thought sent through her chest was numbing, and suddenly China sucked in her breath in astonishment as a disturbing realization washed over her: She was in love with

Byron. Despite all her warnings to herself, she had fallen in love with him. She tried desperately to convince herself that it was only on the rebound, but she knew that wasn't true. For the first time in her life she was really in love. Her experience with Dereck had been nothing compared to the intense, overwhelming emotion she was feeling for Byron, and she was devastated to realize it. She wanted to spend every moment with him, to share her life with him, to be caressed and touched by him forever.

Dereck was well out of her life, she knew, but she had given him up for more heartache. She bitterly recalled Granny saying all things worked out for the best, but she couldn't see how in this case.

She knew that Byron didn't feel the same way she did. Although she told herself she should have been aware of her growing love for him, she hadn't recognized it for what it was until now. She didn't want to be in love with him. It was impossible; it was dangerous; it could only hurt. But now it was too late, way too late. And she was sure to pay with her heart.

CHAPTER TWELVE

At last the meal was over, and while Byron and Duncan sat drinking a glass of whisky, China offered to help Hilliary with the dishes. When the old woman refused, China gratefully excused herself to go upstairs and take a nap. She was suddenly very, very tired, and she knew the realization that she was in love with Byron was only part of the reason for her weariness; the other part was his answer to Hilliary's question.

And yet, what had she expected him to say? That he intended to marry her? She knew it was a lie, and the unhappiness that filled her heart drove her faster and faster up the steps. Finally she flung herself across the bed, and unexpectedly, tears began to seep from her eyes.

She tried to tell herself that it was sheer exhaustion and too much excitement, but she couldn't be sure that it wasn't plain old heartache that caused her to weep.

China was awakened some time later by the soft touch of Byron's lips against hers. She rolled over, still half asleep, and held out her arms. He sat down on the side of the bed, and for a moment China was surprised that he didn't lie down beside her and embrace her. She opened her dark eyes and peered into his gray ones. Then she looked around, remembering where she was.

She was unable to smile, recalling how she had cried herself to sleep. She knew that being here with Byron now would only cause her more pain. It would no longer be enough for her to simply be his lover—not when she was in love with him.

She forced a smile to her lips. He hadn't brought her here under any conditions; he had promised her a good time in Scotland, and suddenly she resolved to do her best to make the most of the trip. She would not waste her tears on him again. She would enjoy this time with him, and when it was over, she would face the future alone.

Seeing the slight curve of her lips, and mistaking her smile for pleasure, Byron lightly kissed her mouth again.

"It's after eight," he told her. "You've been napping for almost an hour. Do you want to keep sleeping, or shall we go back into Edinburgh to sample that nightlife? We still have six days, so you decide what you want to do."

Determinedly putting her unpleasant thoughts behind her, China said, "I'd like to go back to the city."

"Good. I want to take you to a well-known night spot where they have traditional Scottish entertainment. I think you'll enjoy it."

"That sounds wonderful," China agreed, warming to the idea. That was exactly what she needed, something to distract her from her brooding thoughts about this man. And she did want to see everything she possibly could in the six days they would be here. She wouldn't let her secret pain spoil Scotland for her.

"Good. This is your chance to wear one of those nice new outfits, like the one you wore to the lawyer's office. We'll get all done up and do the town. After the show we'll go discotheque-ing until you're too tired to dance."

The mention of that day reminded China of why she was here with this man. She realized how very difficult it would be to share the cabin with him now that she knew how deeply she cared. On the one hand, she still wanted him to sell her his half so she need never see him again; but on the other, the thought of staying there without him was strangely bleak. She would even miss Demon, she realized with a start. The cat and his master had certainly kept things interesting for the past few days.

"That was yesterday," she muttered. "This is today." She had just told herself she was going to enjoy this trip; she had to live for the moment and forget the past. There was nothing like dancing to make her forget her problems, and she hadn't gone dancing in far too long.

"What did you say?" Byron asked.

"I said I love to dance," she improvised.

"You didn't say that," he said. "You were muttering again. I can't tell what's going on with you when you have a conversation with yourself."

China managed to smile. "You're not supposed to."

He tapped her nose playfully. "Do you remember how to get to the bathroom?"

"Yes."

"Oh, damn, I wanted to show you the way." He nuzzled her neck. "I want to shower with you."

China looked into his eyes and saw that they were darkening with passion. She hadn't thought about how much she would miss making love while she was here, and for a moment she was sorry they weren't staying in a hotel.

"Somehow I don't think your grandparents would appreciate that," she murmured.

"They're not here," he said in a husky voice. "They've gone to an ailing friend's house to take her some dinner. They said

166

they won't be gone longer than an hour." He smiled wickedly at her. "That just might be enough time to shower with you."

"You don't know how to stop with just a shower," she teased, trying to be playful. It wasn't Byron's fault she had fallen in love with him. He only wanted to have fun, to show her a good time, and she was going to try to make the best of the situation.

"You're right," he agreed. "I can't seem to get enough of you, China. I want you so much, I ache for you."

He drew her into his arms, and when his mouth lowered to hers, China hadn't the willpower to resist. His magic touch had the power to make her forget everything but him.

She loved him. She wanted him. And although she told herself that she didn't need any more memories of him to haunt her, she couldn't seem to convince her body. She wanted one more magic time with him, one more trip into the depths of desire, one more incomparable journey into love, with all its tantalizing ecstasy and enchantment, with all its lush pleasures and wondrous intimacy.

She savored the exciting kiss, losing herself in the joy and the thrill of Byron's masterful possession of her mouth. He hugged her tightly to his body, molding her breasts to the powerful lines of his chest, and she wrapped her arms around his neck, her fingers caught up in his blond curls.

His mouth left hers to scatter teasing kisses over her eyelids, nose, and cheeks. China closed her eyes and gave herself up to the exquisite sensations Byron was creating in her. She didn't want to think about the future; she wanted only this moment in time with her lover, lost in a world of their own, separated from the realities and disappointments of life.

He began to take her clothes off, and she helped him, her fingers touching his as they unbuttoned her blouse and discarded her bra. Then she raised her hips so that Byron could slip off her slacks. His hands trailed along her skin teasingly, and China smiled at him as she reached out to trace his strong jaw with her fingers. As he slid her bikini panties down her hips he buried his face in the sensitive skin of her abdomen, biting and kissing, setting China on fire. He erotically slid the skimpy piece of silk inch by inch down her thighs, his mouth trailing hot kisses along the path his fingers had just traveled, and

China arched her hips in hungry anticipation of his possession of her.

When Byron had tossed the garment aside, he parted China's legs to kiss the inside of her thighs, and she moaned softly. With his tongue Byron began to make long, broad strokes, licking the sensitive flesh until China trembled uncontrollably.

"Oh, Byron," she said under her breath, reaching out for him. When her hands encountered the cloth barrier that shielded him from her touch, she began to tug at his shirt.

Byron drew back from her so that she could help him undress. Eagerly, quickly, they both stripped off his clothes, and when he, too, was nude, China drew him down on top of her.

He began to spill quick kisses all over her, leaving no part of her untouched in his hunger to taste her skin. His palms moved lightly and rapidly over her breasts, brushing them gently, arousing China to new heights of passion. He caressed her hips and stroked her thighs, sending walls of fire roaring through her veins.

She was so aware of him, his virility, and his passion, and his sensual seduction was so strong and stirring, that she didn't think she could stand any more love play. Already burning for him, she wanted to experience the ultimate satisfaction of having him become one with her.

She drew him back up to her and found his mouth to kiss it passionately. "China, sweet China," he groaned against her parted lips. "I want you. I want you."

Moving away from her, he stood up by the side of the bed. Then he drew China toward him, positioning her at the edge of the mattress. When he had slid her long legs up over his shoulders, he leaned over her, supporting himself with his hands on either side of her.

Then slowly, maddeningly, he possessed her, easing deeper and deeper into her velvety depths, causing her to suck in her breath at the thrill of the union. Arching his powerful hips, he penetrated until China quivered with delicious sensations. She was crazy with desire, the flush of passion heating her body and bathing it in a moist glow as she met Byron's slow thrusts.

Opening her glazed eyes to gaze at him, she saw that he was

watching her, and their eyes locked. When a joyous smile curved her lips, he smiled in return.

With a rhythmic movement that sent a rush of ecstasy spiraling up through China's body, Byron began the journey that would carry them to the heavens. His desire-darkened eyes still holding hers, he deeply stroked her body with his, claiming and caressing the magic and wonder that was she.

Her hands explored his thighs and back, moving faster as Byron's lovemaking gradually increased in intensity. The pace of their passion quickened, and the long, slow strokes became deeper and stronger. He began to move with more urgency, plunging into her well of love, claiming all the treasure that was to be had, taking them both higher and higher until China thought she would explode among the stars in the sky of their desire.

"Oh, Byron," she moaned, her breath catching in her throat. No longer able to hold his gaze, she closed her eyes. Byron arched against her a final time, sending his love into her, and China gripped his hips and cried out her delight.

For a long time they stayed locked in each other's embrace, letting the bright fires of their passion pale to soft contentment. Finally, Byron freed her and lay down on the bed with her. He drew her into his arms, and China rested against his chest, content in a way she had never known.

But the contentment was not to last. As China gradually came back to earth and its realities, she gazed around the room and was suddenly reminded that she was in the Scott home and that Byron's grandparents would soon return.

"I'd better take my shower and get dressed so we can go out," she murmured. "I'll be ready in less than thirty minutes."

Byron was watching her with admiring gray eyes, and when she tried to slip out of his arms, he drew her more tightly to him as if he could not bear to let her go, even for a moment. His eyes burned into hers, their expression unreadable.

"China," he said hoarsely.

She waited, her lips parted in expectation as she willed him to tell her what she badly wanted to hear. His arms closed more tightly around her and she molded herself against him, drawn

169

by the turbulent emotion in his gaze, and as her breasts brushed his chest she felt him tremble slightly.

"Oh, God," he whispered, "I wish you knew. . . ."

"Knew what?" China asked breathlessly.

He opened his mouth as if to speak; then, instead, he leaned down so that his lips were a breath away from hers.

"How very beautiful you are and how much I desire you."

China couldn't help wondering if that was really what he had intended to say. Something told her—whether it was the gleam in his eyes or the soft yearning in his face—that he was holding back. Or had she only wanted to hear something else so desperately that she had imagined he had wanted to say more?

His lips at last touched hers, their melting warmth sending a spiral of desire through her body. Then abruptly he released her. "It is late. If we're going to do the town, we'd better get under way."

She smiled at him, trying her best to hide her disappointment. She had promised herself that she would make the most of her time in Scotland, and making love with Byron here had just been a part of what would become her Scotland memories.

"Yes," she murmured. "Besides, we don't want to miss the show."

Byron pressed her hand closer to his mouth and whispered into her palm, "Nothing can compare with what we've just shared." He freed her, then said, "I'll leave you alone so you can get ready in peace." With a grin he reached for his slacks, pulled them on, gathered up the rest of his clothes, and left.

China watched his retreating figure, a gentle smile on her face. Brushing back her long, dark hair, she made her way to the closet to get her robe. When she had located her shower cap, she went downstairs to the bathroom.

The shower was a handheld one, but as China climbed under the warm spray, she reveled in the refreshing water. She stayed there for a long time, lost in her thoughts, feeling a little guilty, for she had been told that people in Europe didn't waste water the way Americans did. But it felt so wonderful after the long, tiring trip and her time in Byron's arms.

She felt revitalized when she finally stepped out of the tub and dried herself with a thick towel. The thought of the exciting

170

evening ahead with Byron made her face glow in anticipation, and she quickly shook out her hair, pulled on her robe, and hurried back to her room to dress.

Byron's grandparents had returned and were sitting in the living room, talking, when China entered. Dressed in a sleek blue waltz-length dress and fashionable high heels, a white coat over one arm, she looked especially lovely. Her dark hair glistened and swayed as she moved, and when she smiled, her face glowed.

"You look beautiful," Byron murmured, his eyes holding hers. His grandparents echoed his sentiments, and China gave them a throaty laugh.

"Thank you so much," she murmured. She had dressed quickly, but she had known this particular dress was the most gorgeous one she had purchased for her trousseau. Her cheeks turned a little pink at the compliment, adding to her beauty.

"Are you ready?" Byron asked.

China let her sparkling dark eyes briefly assess him before she replied. He was dressed in a new deep-gray suit with a silver shirt that accented his eyes. She couldn't recall when he had looked more handsome. "Whenever you are," she murmured.

"Now, you two stay as late as you like," Grandfather Scott said. "Have a good time."

"We won't be gone long," Byron said. "I suspect our energy will run low after the trip from the States. We'll just sample the nightlife, then come back. But don't wait up for us."

The old couple smiled at each other, then at the young people. "Enjoy yourselves," Hilliary said, her lined eyes beaming.

Taking China's hand, Byron escorted her out the door. "I thought you were beautiful before, but now . . ." For the first time since China had known him, Byron seemed to be at a loss for words. "Scotland certainly agrees with you," he whispered when they were outside.

China laughed again. She had never thought of herself as extremely attractive, but tonight, with Byron by her side, she felt beautiful. "I'm so glad we came," she said. "It's everything I ever dreamed it could be."

"You haven't seen anything yet," he assured her. "We've barely scratched the surface of Edinburgh."

China soon found that he was right. They drove to a hotel where a *ceilidh,* or folk night, was being held, and China enjoyed Scottish dancers and fiddlers who performed in native costumes. When the piper came out to play a haunting Highland tune on his bagpipes, Byron leaned forward and wickedly whispered, "Did you know that it's improper to wear anything under the kilt?"

"I don't believe it," she replied, shaking her head at him.

"It's true," he insisted, and China didn't know if he was teasing or not.

"Why is the piper wearing that pouch?" she asked to change the subject.

"It's called a sporran and it's made of leather. It was once used to carry dry oatmeal. If a Scotsman got hungry, he would immerse a handful of oatmeal in a stream to soften it. Tonight the piper is wearing the sporran only to make tourists like you ask questions."

China lightly slapped him on the shoulder. "I'll bet you asked your share of questions before you got all these answers," she retorted.

Byron laughed. "You bet I did." His eyes held hers for a moment. Then he stood up. "Let's go dancing. You've had enough Scottish history for one day."

Readily agreeing, China followed him from the room.

The discotheque Byron finally located was crowded and lively. The music was a Scottish rendition of some of the latest popular tunes, and China laughed gaily when Byron pulled her out on the small dance floor before they had even found a table.

Sliding his arms into China's white coat, Byron molded his body to hers as he guided her around the floor to a slow-paced tune sung by a group of bearded Scotsmen. China could feel the echo of her own heartbeats as Byron held her to his chest. He looked into her eyes, and there was no mistaking the passion burning so brightly in the grayness of his. She knew that it was matched in her own dark gaze.

Her intense awareness of him brought back that moment in her room earlier, and she was acutely aware of the inexplicable thread that bound them together. The music wrapped them in a special magic, the slow beat pulsing through their bodies, hypnotizing them, holding them in that wondrous state, lost to all but each other. Byron turned her in small circles, making a world for them alone, moving as easily with her as if they had danced a thousand times.

China hoped this time would never end. She loved Byron so much that it was a physical ache inside her. She never wanted to leave his arms, to lose the warmth of him burning against her, stirring all her senses to never-before-attained heights.

But it wasn't long before the music ended, and Byron drawled near China's ear, "We'd better find a table and sit down before I make love to you right here on the dance floor."

China smiled at him, but she trembled as he guided her through the crowd to a small table in a darkened corner of the room. She was flushed with pleasure, and she could feel her eyes glowing as she watched Byron. She had never felt quite this way, and to her chagrin she reminded herself that the feeling was known as love.

Byron held out a chair for her, and when she had sat down, he lightly squeezed her shoulder. "Having fun, beautiful?" he asked.

She nodded, but for a moment she was unable to speak.

The music began again, but Byron ignored the fast tune. "What would you like to drink?" he asked, and China strained to break away from her troubling thoughts and hear his low voice over the loud music. "Would you like to try a rusty nail— malt whisky and a measure of Drambuie—or a Scotch mist— whisky, squeezed lemon rind, and crushed ice? Or, since you're from California earthquake country, maybe you'd like to attempt an earthquake, which contains one-third whisky, one-third gin, and one-third absinthe."

Seeing the frown on China's face, Byron laughed heartily. "I'm teasing. I don't think you're up to the local drinks. How about a—"

China interrupted him. "I *do* think I'm up to them." Perhaps a strong drink was just what she needed, she told herself. "I believe I'll try the Scotch mist. It sounds romantic."

Byron shook his head and grinned at her. "It might *sound* romantic, but it's strong."

"Good. That's just what I need to warm up."

"Oh?" he murmured, sliding his chair around beside hers. "I didn't know you were cold." He wrapped his arm around her shoulders, and China leaned into him.

This man was having the most devastating effect on her, and there was little she could do to counteract it. She *was* looking forward to a strong drink; perhaps it would offset Byron's potent arousal of her senses. She was much too aware of him, especially in this compelling foreign atmosphere. Maybe the Scotch would dull her awareness, mute the excitement that coursed through her body when he looked at her or touched her.

"All right," he said, still smiling. "I like a woman with spirit."

When the waiter came over, Byron ordered a Scotch mist for China and a rusty nail for himself. After they had been served, China boldly took a big drink of hers. It *was* powerful; it burned all the way down her throat, but she wasn't about to tell Byron so. He watched her, laughter in his eyes, as she swallowed and immediately took another drink, this time a smaller one.

She suddenly began to realize just how tired she really was. It had been a long and exciting day, and the drink was bringing her down to earth all too fast. She was getting sleepy, and no matter how she tried to fight it, she could feel her weariness settling in her bones.

"Dance?" Byron murmured.

She shook her head. She couldn't dance if she wanted to. "I hate to be a spoilsport," she muttered, "but I find that I'm utterly exhausted. Would you mind if we went back to the house now?"

"Why, China," he teased, "it's barely after ten."

She tried to laugh, but found she was too weary even for that. "Which country's time?" she murmured, her eyes feeling as heavy as if someone had put lead weights on her lids.

Byron was having no such difficulty, but he downed his drink, then held out his arm to her. "Come on, Sleeping Beauty, it's been a long day for you."

"I really am sorry," she apologized.

"Nonsense," he countered. "It's time we were both in bed. We can start out early tomorrow."

174

"Yes," she agreed, but just then she didn't know if she would even be able to get out of bed the next day. Byron helped her back into her coat and they left quickly.

China hardly remembered the ride back to the village. Byron drew her head down on his shoulder, and lost to her tiredness and his nearness, she dozed. She roused drowsily when Byron parked the car and lifted her in his arms to carry her inside.

"I can walk," she murmured.

He kissed her lips. "I like carrying you," he whispered as he made his way to the house. "I suspect my grandparents are asleep," he told her as he set her on her feet and silently opened the front door.

But he was wrong, and China was suddenly wide awake as she and Byron crept into the house. They were just in time to hear Hilliary say, "Why do you think Byron doesn't marry China? I believe she's in love with him. Don't you think it's just because he can't forget Sara?"

"Good evening, Grandfather, Grandmother," Byron said, his controlled voice effectively silencing the old couple. China could feel her face flame, but she stood where she was, a forced smile on her lips as an unhappy realization swept over her. Byron would *never* marry her. He *couldn't* forget Sara. She knew it as well as his grandmother did.

"Ah, Byron, China, it's early. We didn't expect you back so soon," Duncan said, his face turning a little pink.

"China was tired," Byron explained stiffly.

Miserable, seeing an excuse to flee, China nodded and murmured, "I can hardly stay awake. If you don't mind, I'll just go to bed. Good night." Then she walked out of the room, leaving the uneasy silence behind her. She went upstairs and firmly shut her door. For a few minutes she leaned against it, breathing hard. Hilliary had effectively put into words what China had feared all along, and the old woman's question had left an empty ache in China's heart. She could feel the tears coming to her eyes, and she valiantly fought to suppress them.

She was still leaning against the door when she heard a rap on the other side. "Yes?" she murmured.

"It's Byron. Open the door."

China moved farther into the room, but she couldn't bring

herself to turn the knob. Without waiting, Byron opened the door, stepped inside, then closed it behind him. When he saw her pale face, he clenched his fists.

He wished more than anything that his grandmother hadn't said what she had, but it was done. And he didn't know what to say to China.

"Don't pay any attention to Grandmother," he murmured as he drew her into his arms. "She thinks we would make a good match."

China sighed as he held her against his body. Her own grandmother had thought the same thing, and look at the mess she was in now. Suddenly she wished she were back in the little cabin in Big Sur, all alone. She wished that she had never heard of Byron Scott. But even as the thought occurred to her, she knew it was a lie.

Drawing away from him, she murmured, "I am tired. I'd really like to go to bed now."

Byron stared at her for a moment longer, but he knew she had already withdrawn into her protective shell. He saw the futility of discussing the matter further with her, and anyway, at the moment he really didn't know what to say. He lightly kissed her forehead, then turned away.

When he had closed the door after him, he stood outside for a long time. He couldn't bear to see China upset. He cared for her more than he wanted to admit, even to himself.

His hand tightened painfully on the cold doorknob as he remembered the look on her face when he had held her in his arms earlier that evening. He had been overwhelmed in that instant by a wash of emotions he could not name. But now, as he stood with only the blank face of the door between them, the name came to him clear and vibrant in the still air—love. Despite all his intentions he had fallen in love with China Castleberry.

He wanted to deny his feelings, but he knew there was no point. He could only rail silently at his own weakness. He had promised himself that he wouldn't get caught in that trap again. Love hurt and he had already known enough of that kind of pain. And—dear God!—China wasn't over Dereck yet. She needed time. He needed more time himself. And he intended to see that they both got it.

Finally he walked down to his own room and got ready for bed. But when he had slipped beneath the covers, he found the silence of the room and the loudness of his whirling thoughts overwhelming. Unable to sleep, he made his way back down the hall. For a while he stood uncertainly outside China's room. Then, clenching his fists in frustration, he went down to the living room and poured himself a stiff drink of Scotch.

The next morning China awakened to the wonderful smells of breakfast cooking. She had slept poorly, but she was determined that she would put on a bright front and be pleasant. She didn't want to think about last night again. It hurt too much.

When she had stumbled from the bed, she pulled on her robe and went down to the bath to wash up. Upon her return to her room, she dressed in slacks and a button-down shirt. After brushing her hair and putting on lipstick, she tested her smile, then went down to the kitchen.

Byron, Hilliary, and Duncan turned to look at her when she entered. "Good morning," she said brightly. She saw at once that Byron seemed relieved by her pleasant tone.

Hilliary looked away, embarrassed. "Good morning, lassie," she murmured.

Duncan, too, seemed tense today, and China was especially sorry that she was the source of the couple's discomfort. "Are you well today?" he asked hopefully.

"I feel fine," she answered. "I slept well, and when I awakened to those enticing aromas, I knew it was going to be another grand Scottish day."

Hilliary peeked at her guest again, smiled, and returned to her cooking.

"Sit down," Byron said. "You'll enjoy this. A Scottish breakfast is quite a meal. They believe in a hearty fare to start off the day, and Hilliary is really doing this up right for you." He glanced at his grandmother, then said teasingly, "She cooks almost as well as I do."

China was amazed at how easily her smile came after the night before. But it seemed that the ice had been broken and

177

everyone was visibly relaxing. "May I help with something?" China asked.

The old woman smiled warmly. "No, you're a guest in my house—a most welcome one," she added. "I want to make you comfortable."

"And you have," China said, realizing that the woman was doing her best to apologize for what China had overheard last night. She accepted a cup of tea Byron poured for her and began sipping it contentedly.

Hilliary came to the table with a tray of toast covered with anchovies and scrambled eggs, and China glanced at it with interest.

"That's Scotch woodcock," Byron explained.

The names these Scots come up with, China mused silently.

Next Hilliary set steaming bowls of porridge in front of each of them.

"It's oatmeal porridge," Byron said, "made with salt and served with cream. People here can't imagine anyone eating it with sugar."

Sugar was just what China had had in mind, but she smiled and nodded. She would eat it with the salt as it was intended.

Fruit juice and an assortment of sweet rolls and jams and marmalade completed the meal. Apparently satisfied at last, Hilliary sat down. Soon everyone was eating and talking, the previous night's tense moments deliberately forgotten.

"What are you going to see today?" Duncan asked.

Byron began to list the itinerary: "Greyfriers Bobby, the Royal Mile, the zoo, a local pub—"

"Byron!" Duncan exclaimed, interrupting him, "you'll wear the lassie out. That's too much for one day."

Byron winked at China. "She's up to it. She's a hearty lassie, and she wants to see it all." He wiped his mouth on a linen napkin. "But I do think we'd better be under way if we're to get in a full day. Are you about ready?"

"Yes," China replied. "I'm eager, in fact. And after a delicious breakfast like this, I shouldn't have to eat again today." She glanced at Byron's grandmother. "If Hilliary will let me do the dishes, I'll be on my way."

"No dishes," the woman informed her firmly. "You run ahead and have a good time."

China extended her hands helplessly. "I'd really like to help a little."

"No, no, you two go ahead."

Byron grabbed China's hands and pulled her up. "Let's go," he said. "We have a lot to see."

China's laughter lingered in the air as Byron helped her into her coat and guided her to the rented car. Soon they were once again en route to Edinburgh.

China was enchanted by the story of Greyfriers Bobby, as Byron had predicted, when they went to view the tall bronze statuette of the Skye terrier.

"The dog belonged to Jock Gray, a shepherd who died in 1858," Byron said. "From then until the time of his own death in 1872, the faithful terrier maintained a night-and-day vigil over his beloved master's grave in Greyfriers Churchyard. He became such a legend in his own time that he was given virtual freedom of the city. In fact, he was even made a freeman of the Edinburgh, and Scotsmen will tell you that meant that he had the vote long before women did."

China was so touched by the story that it brought tears to her eyes. She was soon distracted from her sad emotions by the Royal Mile, a sequence of four connecting streets running from Edinburgh Castle to the royal retreat, Holyrood Palace.

The rest of the day went by in a whirl as they visited the zoological park, which covered some eighty acres and included a tropical bird house that caused China to think of Blue. The zoo was fascinating and took up the balance of the day as the couple saw everything from parrots to polar bears.

By the time they had dinner at a well-known restaurant, then stopped for a drink in a colorful pub, night had fallen, and with it the cold. On the way back to the house China snuggled down in her coat and sighed contentedly. She had enjoyed the day tremendously, and she was feeling mellow and happy as she looked at Byron.

"Did you have a good time?" he asked, taking his gaze off the winding road only briefly.

"Marvelous," she replied, smiling. Then she found herself

thinking that all that was missing was Byron's loving to make the day complete.

But to her surprise and dismay he gave her only a light kiss on her lips when they had parked in the drive of his grandparents' house. In fact, the kiss had been almost chaste. Byron had displayed none of the fire and passion he had shown toward China all week, and she didn't know what to think. Was he tiring of her? Had the comment Hilliary made cooled his ardor? China didn't understand, but pride wouldn't allow her to mention his lack of affection.

He had been charming and entertaining all day. She would simply have to settle for that. But she couldn't fight back the wave of disappointment that washed over her as he walked with her to her room, squeezed her hand, then left her. Was their brief affair already over? Had Hilliary's reminder of Sara made him realize that China could never take his ex-wife's place? Had he found that she really was only a friend? Surely it was much too late for that. Or was she the only one who had taken their lovemaking so seriously?

CHAPTER THIRTEEN

The day they visited the zoo seemed to have been a turning point in Byron and China's relationship, a turning point that she didn't understand. He hadn't discussed it, but he had limited his kisses and caresses to precious few after that. By day and evening he and China toured Edinburgh royally, seeing all the sights they could cram into their short visit, from Holyrood Palace to Abbotsford, Sir Walter Scott's baronial mansion. By night they parted at her door with quick kisses and uncertain smiles.

Hilliary and Duncan were delightful, and China grew fond of

them and enjoyed their dry wit a great deal as she came to know them better. She enjoyed seeing the love they shared with their grandson, and she was pleased by Byron's response to it. But she was hurt and perplexed by his lack of affection toward her.

Filled with tours and excitement, the days flew by in rapid succession. All too soon the Scotland dream came to an end, and China began to worry that she would never see Byron again. She wanted to talk to him about their relationship, but she wasn't sure what she wanted to say. And she never seemed to find the right opening to bring the subject up, not even when they finally boarded the plane for the long flight home. Byron seemed lost in his own thoughts, and China sat beside him, wondering what the future would bring.

They had left his car at the airport, and as they drove back toward the little cabin where they had first met, China felt an almost unbearable anxiety building up inside her. Byron still hadn't mentioned the future, and she had begun to wonder if he ever would, when he cleared his throat and broke the silence at last.

"Thanks for going with me, China," he said lightly. "I hope you enjoyed it."

"It was one of the most wonderful times in my life," she replied.

He patted her hands, which were tightly clasped in her lap. "Good. I wanted it to be special for you." He glanced at her, his eyes dark with emotions she could not name, and for an instant she saw a gleam of the old fire there. But Byron quickly quenched the flame.

When he looked back at the road, China could feel her heart breaking. She was sure he was trying to tell her that he wouldn't be seeing her again. Was this all there was to be? Several wondrous times in his arms and a quick trip to Scotland? It couldn't be, not when he had changed her entire life. Her love for him had only grown stronger with the passage of each day. Was he really going to walk away now without a backward glance?

He spoke again, and China realized that he was. "I'll be leaving first thing in the morning," he said quietly.

She could hardly keep herself from asking if she would ever see him again, but she kept quiet as he searched for the words to express his troubled thoughts. It was a long and agonizing time before he continued.

"I know that we came into each other's lives at a bad time, China," he said gently. "You still care for Dereck very much, don't you?"

She bit down on her lower lip. How could he believe that, after all they had shared? Was he really so blind? If so, then he probably never would understand her love for him, nor could he return it. She had thought, once or twice, that he had come to care for her, too, but she saw that she had been mistaken. She couldn't compare to Sara.

"Yes," she said, trying not to choke on the lie. "I do. I can't fall in and out of love as easily as you apparently can. I can't sweep one man away one day and let another into my heart the next."

He stared at her with stormy eyes for a moment, stunned by the pain that left him speechless. Yet, it was no more than he had expected. He had rushed her. He hadn't given her enough time to heal from the pain of loving Dereck, and although the fact hurt him much more than he had thought it would, he knew he would have to accept it. He loved China too much to let his desire tear her apart inside.

He nodded, and China compressed her lips into a tight line to stop them from quivering. She could feel the tears rising to her eyes, and she had promised herself that she wouldn't cry. Hadn't she learned her bitter lesson from Dereck? Obviously not, she cried silently.

"I understand how you feel," Byron said at last.

China looked away. He didn't understand, and she knew he never would. She was in love with him, for all the good it did her. But she would not give him the satisfaction of knowing that. She would go back to Palm Springs and forget him. Somehow.

They fell silent as they worked their way back into the hills of Big Sur, and when Byron stopped the car, China hurried to open the front door. Everything looked just as they had left it. The couch was a mute reminder of all the times Byron had

182

taken her in his arms there. The sight of the bed caused a bittersweet memory to rise vividly in her mind. How empty this cabin would be without Byron, how echoing and cold the rooms.

China made her way to the guest room, and when she heard Byron bring the suitcases inside, she went to retrieve hers. She would leave tomorrow too. She had realized in an instant that she could not bear to stay here without him.

When she had dragged her suitcase into her room, she turned to Byron, who was watching her from the doorway. "I'm going down to Karly's to pick up Blue."

"Shall I go with you?"

She shook her head. "No, thanks." She didn't want to spend any more time with him than she could help; she didn't want to make more memories to forget.

He silently watched her as she brushed past him and moved toward the back door. Then he went into Granny's room and began to get ready for the trip back home in the morning. He wanted to leave before China got up. He didn't think he could bear to tell her good-bye. It was one thing to think about giving her more time to reassess her life, but actually doing it would prove very difficult.

China stayed at Karly's for a long time despite her depression and exhaustion. The old couple wanted to hear all about the trip, and China told them all the wonderful moments, leaving out the painful ones. She realized as she talked just how much Byron had meant to her, how much she had enjoyed him.

His sense of humor was rare, and she could not forget the sensitivity he had often displayed toward her. Just for a moment, caught in the web of romance and wonder that had been Scotland, she thought he had begun to understand her. But now she knew he had not. The thought brought a dull ache that began in her chest and spread slowly outward.

Despite the fact that she had known him for so short a time, she could not imagine living without his warm smile and his laughing gray eyes. But she would have to learn.

The hurt was building inside her until it threatened to explode, and finally she took Blue and returned to the house. The

183

door to Granny's room was shut, and China crept past it to her own.

Blue, happy to be back home, was squawking boisterously, calling out "Thanks a lot," but China barely heard him. She could hear little over the painful beating of her aching heart, and she could think of little beyond the man in the next room. Why had she been a fool and fallen in love with him?

She shook her fist at the ceiling. "Damn you, Granny," she muttered bitterly. "Now look what you've gone and done." But Granny hadn't done this at all, China knew. Granny had only wanted her granddaughter's happiness. She hadn't known that it would be impossible with a man like Byron Scott.

China awakened early the next morning, but it wasn't early enough to see Byron off. Irritable, unhappy, she took Blue down the hall to the kitchen. A pot of water was still warm on the stove, and a note was propped up on the counter.

"Will stay in touch. Take good care of yourself, and be careful going home. Love, Byron."

"Love, Byron," China muttered to herself. "Love, Byron."

The phrase caught Blue's fancy, and he repeated it mockingly: "Love Byron. Love Byron."

"Yes," China snapped at him. "I love Byron, for all the damn good it does me." She balled her hands into fists, blinking to fight back her tears, but it was a losing battle. Suddenly they began to stream down her cheeks. China slumped down in a chair and rested her arms on the table. "Oh, why? Why?" she cried.

But Blue, watching curiously from his cage, had no answer this time.

The tourist season was going strong when China returned to Palm Springs, and she found that business was more brisk than ever. For once she was happy to put in all those additional hours at work; it helped her forget the aching misery she was feeling inside.

The days began to follow one after another, and soon a week had passed. China heard nothing at all from Byron—not that it

184

had surprised her, but her foolish heart had not given up hope that she wouldn't be so easily forgotten.

Still another week was to pass before China heard Byron's voice on her answering machine. She had just come in the door from work as he was leaving a message. She stopped where she was, listening, her heart pounding.

"This is Byron," he said, as if she wouldn't know. "I was thinking about you. I hope everything's all right."

China went over to stand by the phone, unsure of whether she wanted to pick up the receiver or not, but when Byron spoke again, she let her hand fall to her side.

"I'd like to talk with you," he said. There was another pause. "We still have to decide what to do about the cabin."

"Yes, the cabin," she muttered bitterly. The one tie that still held them together.

There was another pause, and before Byron could speak, the machine cut him off. It was set for a forty-five-second message and his time had ended. China waited, wondering if he would call back, but he didn't.

For a long time she stood there, staring at the phone, thinking. And as she did she made a difficult decision: She didn't want any ties to Byron Scott. She realized that now. There was no point in it; owning the cabin with him would always be a painful reminder that she was in love with him—and that he didn't return that love. She would spend one more weekend there and then she would contact the lawyer in Monterey about selling her half to Byron.

She would never again be able to stay there without thinking about Byron, but she wanted one last time with her memories and her thoughts, one last time to sort out her life. She would get a weekend, no matter what it took, and she would spend it there with Blue.

It was yet another week before China was able to get away. In the meantime Byron called her twice more, but she didn't return his calls. What would have been the point?

The trip to the cabin was long and wearisome, despite the gorgeous scenery and Blue's caustic comments on the way up. China was filled with both sorrow and happiness when she finally pulled up in the driveway. This place held so many memories for her of her grandparents, of Byron, of times both happy and sad.

She was glad that evening was falling. Soon she could just go to bed and forget all her unhappiness. She settled in with her luggage and Blue, then went over to let the Davises know she had come up. Karly insisted that she have dinner with them and she gratefully accepted. She didn't feel like cooking for herself that night.

It was almost eight when she went back to the lonely cabin. Blue had long since gone to sleep, perched on one foot, his feathers fluffed out for warmth. China quietly covered his cage, then changed into her nightclothes. She hadn't been able to wear her lovely gowns since she had worn them for Byron. Tonight she donned an old flannel nightshirt that had seen better days. It suited her mood precisely. She bundled up under the covers and then waited a long, long time for sleep to overtake her.

The next morning China woke up determined to make the most of her remaining time in the cabin, but it was no easy task. Her memories followed her from room to room, haunting, tormenting, reminding her of her loss even more acutely than she had felt it in Palm Springs, and then she had thought it had been almost unbearable.

Realizing the futility of remaining at the cabin, she called Lloyd Thomas to investigate the possibility of selling to Byron, but to her dismay she found that Lloyd wouldn't be available until Monday. Sighing, she hung up the phone. This would have to be handled long distance. She would not come to the cabin again. She hurt too much here. The center of her being seemed to be her aching heart, and she couldn't stand the pain. She would remain here one more night; in the morning she would leave with the sun, never to return.

Each hour seemed to drag by with painful slowness, but at last dusk streaked the sky with golds, reds, and pinks. It was the excuse China was waiting for to put on her old nightshirt. At the first sign of darkness she was going to have a cup of soup, then go to bed. When she had changed into her nightwear, she returned to the living room. For a long time she

186

stared blindly out the window, oblivious to Blue's chatter as he played on his perch nearby.

When she saw a car coming up the dirt road, it registered only remotely in her mind. She had no interest in who traveled the road or why. But the car came all the way to her house. And then it stopped. Her eyesight became keen as she watched the tall blond man step out of the Rolls-Royce, and her pulse began to pound alarmingly.

Byron! she thought wildly. She pressed her palms against the cool windows and watched as he made his way up the path to the front door, and her heart beat frantically as she waited for the sound of his key in the lock. He wouldn't be expecting her. Her car was parked in the garage. She was sure he wouldn't have come if he had known she was here—but oh, how the sight of him thrilled her foolish heart.

To her surprise he rapped once, then opened the door. China waited breathlessly for him to come inside. It wasn't until she brushed nervously at her hair that she even remembered that she was attired in the old flannel nightshirt. And then it was too late. Byron walked into the room.

"Hello, China," he said smoothly, as if three weeks hadn't passed since they had last seen each other, as if she hadn't suffered a hundred painful heartaches because of him.

"What are you doing here, Byron?" she murmured, trying to get control of her frantic emotions. She hugged her arms to her body and drank in the sight of the man standing before her. It seemed like months instead of weeks since she had seen him.

"Aren't I welcome?" he asked, his voice teasing as he appraised her from head to foot. "You don't seem to be waiting for anyone."

She gestured wildly toward her nightshirt. "I didn't expect you to come."

"I didn't think you would," he drawled. "But I rather like you dressed like that. I never could keep a sane thought in my head when you wore those sexy gowns."

Unable to think of a single thing to say, China simply stared at him. Suddenly it dawned on her that Byron must have been phoning her to let her know he wanted to come up for the

187

weekend; he had wanted to let her know so that she wouldn't be here too. Her face brightened with color.

He rubbed his hands together briskly. "It's a little cold out. Am I welcome to stay?"

"It's your house too," she said bitterly. "Of course you are."

"I'd rather you let me stay because you're happy to see me," he murmured softly as he moved nearer to her.

"I don't think you're exactly happy to see me," she retorted, trying to keep her tone light.

"Why not? I knew you were here."

"You did?" she murmured, puzzled.

"Yes. I went all the way to Palm Springs, trying to catch you at home or at the shops."

"You did?" China couldn't believe it. "And then you came here?"

Byron laughed lightly. "I'm not a ghost. I'm here in the flesh."

China traced the side of her face with a trembling hand. "I don't understand. I thought—I thought—"

"*What* did you think?"

She turned around to face the dancing flames of the fire. "I thought you didn't want to see me again."

She could feel the heat of his body as he moved up behind her, and when he put his fingers on her shoulders, she shivered. "Now you're the one with rocks in your head," he whispered. "I've been so hungry to see you that I could taste it. You're all I've thought about. But you wouldn't even return my phone calls."

She trembled when he kissed her neck. "I thought you were only interested in the cabin," she said quietly.

"I was trying to give you a little breathing space, to let you get over Dereck," he murmured, his breath warm against her ear, "but I couldn't stay away from you."

China turned around to face him. "You couldn't?"

Byron laughed gently. "What are you, a parrot? I told you I couldn't. I love you, China. I didn't want to rush you, but I couldn't let you get away from me. I still can't take that chance. I want you to marry me."

"You want me to marry you," she repeated inanely. Then she realized that she was still parroting him. "I didn't know."

"Of course you didn't. I didn't know myself. I was too afraid of marriage to even consider it. Because of Sara," he said, with no trace of bitterness in his voice. "That was her legacy to me. She married me, then broke my young and vulnerable heart by sleeping with another man. I didn't expect ever to take that risk again." His gray eyes searched her glistening dark ones. "I wouldn't be willing to if I hadn't met you, China. Say that you care for me. Say that you won't let Dereck do to you what Sara did to me for all these years."

China shook her head, and Byron grasped her shoulders, "Don't say no, China," he said forcefully. "Give it some thought before you let what we have go."

China began to laugh. "Oh, Byron, I'm not saying no. I love you so much that it hurts. I'm shaking my head because I just can't believe this. I don't still love Dereck." She laughed softly again. "I don't think I ever did." She gazed into his questioning eyes. "I didn't know what love was until you came into my life. I think I've loved you from the first time you kissed me."

His voice was husky as he drew her into his arms. "You're going to love me a whole lot more, I promise you that. Your Granny was right. You and I were meant for each other. I'm going to make you so happy that you won't know another man ever existed."

Blue, apparently deciding he wanted some attention, too, piped up. "You're young, you'll get over it."

"I sure hope not," Byron said. He glanced at the bird. "That reminds me—we've solved one of our pet problems. Dad kept Demon. He had thought the cat would be a painful reminder of my mother, but he discovered that he found comfort in him. He asked to keep him and I couldn't refuse. Now all we have to do is find a mate for Blue, and the four of us will live happily ever after." He lowered his head to lift a kiss from China's parted lips. "I promise you that."

They both started when Blue suddenly flew off his perch and landed on Byron's shoulder. "Thanks a lot," he cooed. "Thanks a lot."

"See," Byron murmured. "He's grateful I've suggested he get a mate."

"Do you want a bunch of little parrots running around?" China asked with a gleam in her eyes.

"You bet," he retorted quickly. "And a bunch of little babies too. Will you marry me?"

"Oh, yes, Byron. I love you," she whispered. She reached up and wrapped her arms around his neck, but before she could kiss him, Blue hopped over on her shoulder.

"Love Byron. Love Byron," he cooed.

"See, even *he* knew," China said.

"Of course he did," Byron agreed. "He belonged to your granny, didn't he?"

They laughed together before their lips met to still their laughter. Blue flew back to his perch, still calling out, "Love Byron. Love Byron."

China drew away from Byron to whisper, "Forever and always." Then Byron pulled her back into his embrace.

All-new
Candlelight Newsletter

An exceptional, *free* offer awaits readers of Dell's incomparable Candlelight Ecstasy and Supreme Romances.

Subscribe to our all-new CANDLELIGHT NEWSLETTER and you will receive—at absolutely no cost to you—exciting, exclusive information about today's finest romance novels and novelists. You'll be part of a select group to receive sneak previews of upcoming Candlelight Romances, well in advance of publication.

You'll also go behind the scenes to "meet" our Ecstasy and Supreme authors, learning firsthand where they get their ideas and how they made it to the top. News of author appearances and events will be detailed, as well. And contributions from the Candlelight editor will give you the inside scoop on how she makes her decisions about what to publish—and how *you* can try your hand at writing an Ecstasy or Supreme.

You'll find all this and more in Dell's CANDLELIGHT NEWSLETTER. And best of all, *it costs you nothing*. That's right! It's Dell's way of thanking our loyal Candlelight readers and of adding another dimension to your reading enjoyment.

Just fill out the coupon below, return it to us, and look forward to receiving the first of many CANDLELIGHT NEWS-LETTERS—overflowing with the kind of excitement that only enhances our romances!

Now you can reserve January's
Candlelights
<u>before</u> they're published!

♥ You'll have copies set aside for *you* the instant they come off press.

♥ You'll save yourself precious shopping time by arranging for *home delivery.*

♥ You'll feel proud and efficient about organizing a system that *guarantees* delivery.

♥ You'll avoid the disappointment of not finding *every* title you want and need.

ECSTASY SUPREMES $2.50 *each*

☐ **57 HIDDEN MANEUVERS,** Eleanor Woods 13595-8-13
☐ **58 LOVE HAS MANY VOICES,**
Linda Randall Wisdom 15008-6-50
☐ **59 ALL THE RIGHT MOVES,** JoAnna Brandon........10130-1-37
☐ **60 FINDERS KEEPERS,** Candice Adams 12509-X-28

ECSTASY ROMANCES $1.95 *each*

☐ **298 MY KIND OF LOVE,** Barbara Andrews 16202-5-29
☐ **299 SHENANDOAH SUMMER,**
Samantha Hughes 18045-7-18
☐ **300 STAND STILL THE MOMENT,**
Margaret Dobson 18197-6-22
☐ **301 NOT TOO PERFECT,** Candice Adams...............16451-6-19
☐ **302 LAUGHTER'S WAY,** Paula Hamilton...................14712-3-19
☐ **303 TOMORROW'S PROMISE,** Emily Elliott...............18737-0-45
☐ **304 PULLING THE STRINGS,** Alison Tyler 17180-6-23
☐ **305 FIRE AND ICE,** Anna Hudson 12690-8-27